DRYING THE BONES

D1253073

DRYING THE BONES

madeline sonik

NIGHTWOOD EDITIONS

Copyright © 2000 Madeline Sonik
All rights reserved. No part of this publication may be repro-
duced, stored in a retrieval system or transmitted, in any form or
by any means, without prior permission of the publisher or, in the
case of photocopying or other reprographic copying, a licence
from CANCOPY (Canadian Reprography Collective), 214 King
Street West, Toronto, Ontario, M5H 3S6

Nightwood Editions
R.R.#22, 3692 Beach Avenue
Roberts Creek, BC Canada V0N 2W2

We acknowledge the financial support of the Government of
Canada through the Book Publishing Industry Development
Program for our publishing activities. We further acknowledge the
support of the Canada Council for the Arts and the Province of
British Columbia through the British Columbia Arts Council for
our publishing program.

THE CANADA COUNCIL | LE CONSEIL DES ARTS
FOR THE ARTS | DU CANADA
SINCE 1957 | DEPUIS 1957

Cover photograph, cover and interior design by
Martin Nichols, Lionheart Graphics

Canadian Cataloguing in Publication Data

Sonik, Madeline, 1960–
    Drying the bones

    ISBN 0-88971-240-9

    I. Title.
PS8587.O558D79 2000   C813'.6 C00-910765-7
PR9199.3.S573D79 2000

For the best and dearest—
Eric, Madeline and Dyana

Acknowledgements: Some of these stories have previously appeared in *Grain, New Blood & Aphorisms, The Dalhousie Review, Other Voices, Room of One's Own, Wascana Review,* and *Windsor Review.* I would like to thank the Canada Council for its support in the creation of this collection.

CONTENTS

THE BEACON

The forest spirits made themselves plain in the rusty cedars, and we learned to taste life, whole and sweet, from the laddering vines of the salmonberry. When we were young, my sister and brothers and cousins, we all lived wild. We didn't know to want anything. But now, Nathan and me glide across the inlet to the town. He has grown into a man like our father. He is strong and dark and round, and wears a blue peaked cap with the name of the company he works for stitched on: "Pacific Tours." The company also owns this boat, which Nathan uses as if it were his own.

The noisy engine drowns my recollections, and Nathan, smiling, opens a couple of beers.

"Go ahead," he pushes a bottle toward me. His voice is rough from smoking. He flicks the scraggy butt into the water, sighs, "It makes work easier, eh?"

Although I swore I wouldn't, I tilt the brown bottle back, taste the sour explosion of foam in my dry mouth, feel my stiff spine give like a willow branch.

"You're bad," I whisper, take another hit, sit back, drink, see his dark square fingers clutch his bottle. I think about the tree house we had when we were kids— really more like a nest, all padded, feathery hemlock— we curled there watching grown-ups on the beach below kiss the glass lips of brown bottles, cut into the night with their voices. Sometimes they'd be spinning like half shells in the wind. Spinning, then holding real still, as if by stopping they could stop all things. And then when we got older, too big for the nest, we drank too. Drank and drank, until the whole world turned upside down, and you had to lie quiet in the cool, wet sand so you wouldn't fall off or lose your guts, or both.

I want to ask Nathan if he remembers the night Shawna stole those bottles of whiskey from Uncle Ernie. We all went down by the rocks and had ourselves a party. It was the first time I ever got drunk, and Nathan and Trevor decided to go skinny-dipping and almost drowned. I think of these times more often now that I work in town. Nathan brings me across every day. We're the only two left who remember. Our sister and brother are gone. Maureen went to Alberta after she lost custody of her son. Greg's in jail in Kingston, Ontario. Our cousins all went, one by one, to Vancouver: Shawna, Trevor and Clara. They all got hungry for something. I don't know what. We don't hear from them. But Uncle Ernie went to Vancouver once and swears he saw Shawna. He said white guys lay money at her feet while she spins and dances on a table, naked as a worm.

Nathan rolls and lights a joint, takes a toke and passes it. Yesterday, he says, he took six American tourists out whale watching. The water was so rough and pitching, it was like riding over black mountains. He took them way out, cut the engine as soon as he spotted a couple of gray whales, and just let the boat seesaw. A woman in dark glasses and a Cowichan sweater got sick. He gave her a bucket. Then all the others started to feel it too. He kept them out there for an hour, pretending he didn't notice every one of them barfing into the chuck, feeling like they were going to die. It was some joke for forty bucks a head.

He takes a deep draught off his beer now and his mouth pulls into a grin. "You want another beer?" he asks.

I hand him the joint, chug what I have left of the beer, feel relaxed. I try to think of a work-related story I can tell him, where the joke was not on me. This is the kind of story I know he both wants and expects, but the only pictures that come to mind are not ones like these.

He tells me how all the tourists only want to see orcas now anyway. "Shamu, Sea World, and all that crap. They want to pull up right fuckin' next to them and pet their fins."

I take the beer he hands me. I can tell by the sharpness of his eyes he's getting a little crazy.

"I'll never take them out there, even though I know where to find them. One or two grays are good enough—fifty fuckin' feet of bumps and barnacles. No idiot wants to get too close."

He hands me the joint. I take a toke, shut my eyes, press the back of my head against the cold window. I see the tiny space I work in. The posters of honey-skinned blondes with big tits, the telephone.

My own desperate voice echoes in my head but sounds like it belongs to another person. My mother stopped drinking for a month so she could buy me clothes for the interview. I hear her telling Aunt Rose, when she offers a beer, how she never did anything with her life but stayed on the island, had babies, looked after her sister's kids.

I smile at the boss when he says he likes my sexy voice, but my hair's too black to work the front desk. He gets me to make telephone calls at the back where no one can see me but him.

I call old clients and pretend I want to know how they like the studio; then I try to sell them four hundred more minutes of tanning time. Sometimes they hang up. Sometimes they put me on hold until I hang up. If they say they'll buy and then come in and do it, I'm supposed to get a ten percent commission.

He strokes my too-black hair, drops his hand on my shoulder. Mostly he says he's happy with my work.

"If I were a whale, you know what I'd do?" Nathan says. "I'd get all the other whales, and say, 'brothers and sisters, let's get rid of these fuckin', stupid, meddling tourists,' and we'd knock over every goddamned boat in the ocean."

I see my boss's old, gentle face, those vertical creases around his mouth, his tense, shy movements. "Call me

Fred," he says. His white hand steadies my swaying body, touches my thigh. He talks softly like we're making love. "If you come to work pissed like this again, you won't have a job."

He tells me to go into one of the tanning stalls. I can't stop shaking while I wait for him. I look around, see the tanning bed as a fiery white coffin, feel the rough red carpet fibres rip my knees. He smiles, undoes his fly, lets his pants drop over his ankles. No matter how much beer I drink afterwards, I can't get rid of his taste.

When I open my eyes again, everything is blurred and bright. Nathan, whose legs have turned rubbery, has a brilliant yellow halo. The sun glimmers through the beer bottle he passes. It's like watching a film, broken and pieced together. The sky has become a cartoon of coral and azure, and we are running in a different direction.

"Pretty good shit, eh?" Nathan croaks. I feel as if I'm being tickled by thousands of tiny invisible fingers and start to laugh. Nathan laughs too. His face is like a mask. Rubbery, smooth, stretching over teeth he doesn't have. "To hell with work, eh? To hell with work!"

I don't know how many times he repeats it. The words melt together, blend with the thrum of the engine, turn into speed and light. I find another joint between my fingers, suck the sweet searing smoke down into my lungs and hold it there till I choke.

I wash away the ache with beer and watch Nathan's movements, a series of flickering frames. His square hand jerks toward his head; it yanks at his Pacific Tours hat and hurls it into an undertow of misty air. The hat rises and spins, like a whirling seed, and then makes one gigantic loop in its descent to the water, landing like a perfect bubble. In a moment, it's gone.

When I see Nathan next, he is lying like a beached starfish on the deck. The boat has become an oscillating island. Above us, the liquid sky swings and wheels, and Nathan taps the teetering surface beside him with an index finger. My cloudy mind fights to understand. It could be Morse code, or just something to stop him from puking, or maybe a signal to me to lie beside him in the only steady place in the world.

My stomach vaults, I lean over the bow to heave and find myself frigidly sober. Salty dark water slaps my face. We're spinning in the middle of nowhere. It seems as if we always have been.

Nathan's voice grinds out some toneless call. I drop my head between my knees, strain to listen. Rising from the black water is a series of whistles, long and shrill. A stack of misty water shoots over the starboard bow like a geyser. Nathan's eyes roll and flicker in their attempt to stay open. I pull myself to wobbling feet, count five dorsal fins, glistening like wet granite beside us. One whale lifts a dome-shaped head, straight and graceful, out of the water, makes squawking sounds, then rolls on her back, displaying a brilliant belly. Another leaps into the air, the white of her massive body resembling lightning.

My hands reach instinctively for the buttons of my interview sweater. I kick my sandals off, unzip, and slide out of my straight, confining skirt and crouch on the undulating bench, before I lift myself to dive. Nathan's face is turned toward me. His eyes are wide, red-rimmed.

For a moment, the blackness of the ocean swirls beneath, then hungrily consumes. Its sudden shocking cold numbs and erases. When I emerge from the darkness, I reach toward the orca, who stands on her tail and calls, her broad open body the only stable post in this whirling vortex.

GOING EAST

He sent the letter not knowing it would reach me. The envelope, periwinkle blue, is torn in one corner and ragged. There is a circular coffee stain on the back, and black and blue ink of various shades on the front. I can see four of the forwarding addresses, scrawled by strangers from other provinces. The letter, however, originates from Ontario.

I turn it several times in my hands seeing pictures of Windsor in my mind: patchy old roads; treeless, sloping, pale green parks littered with glistening bottle glass; silver chain link fences; subdivisions.

I smell the pungent creosote of the railroad tracks behind our house, see the factories bleed inky black smoke into greying clouds across the Detroit River, and feel gravel hit my legs like buckshot as I read my mother is dying.

My brother came across an address scribbled on a crumpled card. He didn't know, after all these years, if I would still be there, or even for sure if the address had ever been mine. But the letter found me, like a dart. It pins the small red centre of my soul to its pages and fills me with poison.

I'd left that address with her almost a decade ago. I carefully constructed a trail for her to follow all the way across the country. In the beginning, I thought about her every day, waited for her letter and believed she might materialize at any moment begging me to go back with her. I didn't want to give up hope, even later, when it died. But I finally had to.

I couldn't make it live again, and dead it threatened to bury me. I hold a scalding cup of tea. The cool breeze rolls in off the ocean and creates a steamy cloud.

Yesterday I had no past. Like an amniotic sac, like a chrysalis, all traces of Windsor had slipped away. It would be easy to burn the letter, to sit by my window as the city of Victoria rains, and watch people without umbrellas stroll the sea wall, but already I see my mother in the face of every stranger.

At night I dream she is drowning. I hear her voice, amputated and urgent. I am too far to rescue. Diesel fumes and the odour of anticipation surround us. We will travel through the nights, relentlessly and comfortless, stopping only for moments, behind schedule. Through the crumbling mountains, down the threading, black highways, past the barren flat fields.

The driver spins his large wheel as if it were destiny. His caffeine-wired body shifts left and right. Time is running out, it races faster than we do.

Eyes flicker and close. Silent movies. Cocoons. An

embryo. Panting black horses. A casket in a travelling tomb. My mother in a riding cape.

The bus lurches, a child throws up, eyes flicker and open, the bus stops somewhere we have all lost track of. We are told to transfer. We trust. For three days, there is no real sleep, only clipped memories and hallucinations. By the time we reach Windsor, I have lost even this.

The streets smell of searing meat. When I was younger, I walked barefoot here. The tough flesh of my soles surrendered like wax and melted into the tarmac. But I believe now this city claimed more.

There are people on this bus going home. A woman in a flowered sun dress carrying a basket of Okanagan fruit on her lap, an uneasy man. They are going home. Their faces are marked with expressions of this city. Like an accent, they never completely fade. I look at my reflection in the window. My hair is dishevelled, my eyes puffy from sleepless days and nights, but like a birthmark the expression exists here too.

The bus pulls into the terminal. The same small terminal where I once spent a night waiting for a bus going anywhere. The passengers stand before we have fully stopped. I have spent this journey a prisoner of forced air and am surprised to feel the sun wash over me like a tidal wave of molten lava. I yearn for the ocean I have left behind. A hand grabs my elbow.

"How was the trip?" It's my brother's voice. He has become an adult and wears the expression of this city. Polite conversation, smiling, awkward silences. He has become an adult, and I am at a loss for knowing what to say to him.

We drive in his second-hand burgundy Ford through once-familiar streets that now seem shrunken. His smile is fixed as he recounts, like some morbid tour guide, the history of this neighbourhood. Friends and enemies, moved and married, houses built and burned down, children born and unborn tumble together in a collage of images. He tells me at the four-way stop that Mr. Benn, a man who lived at the end of our street, got hit by a car here and spent sixteen days in a coma before finally slipping away.

He has not mentioned our mother, and in an uncomfortable moment that unfolds like the history of this neighbourhood, I know his helplessness.

She is propped up in bed. The room is dark, the curtains drawn. There is a blue pitcher of water at her bedside, and a small thin glass, which she has strength to lift to her dry lips. Her body curls under the blankets, and I am reminded of butterflies that die in their cocoons. She doesn't recognize me, but asks me to come to her. Her hands are cold and dry and small. I touch them, but it is as if something invisible surrounding them does not allow either of us to feel. She looks so deeply into my face it frightens me. I want to turn my head, follow the long cracks in the plaster wall, but I'm fascinated by her intensity—fascinated also by what I recognize to be my own features, emaciated, distorted and foreign.

Before I went west, I thought about meeting her

again, the allegations and the recriminations. I saw
myself stomping out of her house, slamming the door. I
imagined arguments, discussions, conversations and
forgiveness, but I had never imagined this. It is as if all
the dramas of life wither under death. Things have
become suddenly simple. Although I sit here on her bed,
there is more distance now between us than the miles I
put there. Distance enough to see the woman who once
contained me. She is a separate leaf, we are no longer
one plant. She lifts her hand to touch my face. Her
mouth is dry, her breath like dust. "Beautiful," she says,
"always beautiful."

I am young again, watching her put her hair up in the
oval mirror and apply her lipstick. She wears high-heeled
shoes that clip across the floors when she walks. She is
always hurrying and I am always running behind her.
She talks incessantly to the air in front of her, the words
trickle back to me, sometimes wounded, with missing
vowels and crushed consonants. I don't have to understand. They are a leash and collar around my neck.
When she turns and looks at me, I know I am nothing.

It is a sweltering day like today and we are outside on
the patio. She has dressed me in a lacy white dress,
which has taken her weeks to make. It is too tight
around my chest. The inner threads touch me like red
ants. She's baked a white cake with white frosting and
pink icing sugar roses. Her teeth are white and even.
She tells me to stand still and smile for the photographs;
by the time she is finished taking them, the roses are
small red puddles.

In the corner of her room, there is a crumbling cardboard box of photographs. There are pictures of me and my mother, standing together by the Ambassador Bridge. Her hand is balanced on my shoulder, her head cocked to one side. I am wearing a pair of shorts, and she is wearing a dress made out of the same flowered material. Picture after picture finds us smiling. If a stranger discovered these photos, the story they would piece together would be shadowless.

I rifle through the pictures as if I am searching for something valuable to steal. When I lived here, I would have felt it my right to take all of them, but would have been attracted only to those she called "flattering"; now I feel as if I have no rights here at all and am desperate to find only one that is real.

Her sharp cough unnerves me. I drop the photos. Her face ripples with pain and I see her chest heaving as she struggles to breathe. I call the nurse my brother has hired. She cradles my mother's head, pours bright yellow syrup into her mouth. My mother's wasted body thrashes beneath thin blankets. When the nurse leaves, my mother cries.

All night she is restless. I lie on the living room couch, listening to her bedclothes rustle and murmur, wondering why I came. I dream I am a bridesmaid at her wedding, the guests have assembled, music is playing, my mother stands waiting at the altar, but no groom arrives.

There is a wicked place between sleep and wakefulness where we remember—my mother's long white dress and satin shoes and the ten dollar bill he gave me not to tell her, held in my fist, with a bouquet of baby's breath. When they kiss, I feel my stomach shake. He holds me on his lap like a captive. He paralyzes me with words: "Be nice." He unbuttons the dress she has made for me. I am numb. "It would break her heart if you told...."

I lie awake and hear her breath rattle. She cannot console me. The nurse goes home to her family at night. My brother sleeps upstairs. He still has a room in this house he is trying to outgrow—full of baseball cards and model airplanes. I wonder if I should wake him, if we should sink together on this soft couch with our hands clasped on our laps. Instead, I go to the cabinet for my mother's medication alone and fill the small plastic cup with precious yellow syrup.

Her mind is already dead. It has been poisoned by drugs, melted by radiation, drowned by alcohol and years of denial; her consciousness consists only of pain. Her eyes reach a point on the wall behind me, but her mouth takes the medication like desert water and searches for more. I administer another small cup, thinking how easy it would be to end her suffering, but halting myself as I consider all the things that could have prevented suffering if I hadn't been so cowardly.

Her body releases its pain for a moment. Her feverish eyes move back and forth behind their lids. This woman, once strong enough to contain me, more fragile now than a new flame. I could blow her out with one light breath and set her free—the power and desire to do so frighten me.

I pull a chrome chair next to her bed. When I was little and scared, before she met the man, I would have crawled in beside her. She would ask me about my dreams, and I, half-yawning, would watch the nightmares break like cloud and vanish out of reach of words.

A lonely train whistles and I hold her dry hand. I see myself young. I am barefoot, wearing a checkered shirt and jeans. My hair is cropped like a boy's and I am breathless and racing the train. The man who married my mother has left. Said he was going east. My mother's pillow is wet with tears, alcohol, vomit. She doesn't buy food or milk, doesn't even get dressed. She walks to the liquor store in her housecoat and spends welfare money.

I'm running for the train. My mother's man has to come back. I have to threaten him—say I will tell everybody if he forgets what he promised. The train whistles. My brain vibrates. Sticky, smoky pieces of sharp gravel slice my feet as they land. I have never run this fast in my life and finally reach the engine.

I wave my arms at the engineer. His face is frowning, distraught. "Get away from the tracks," I can read his lips—he is so precise. I wave my arms, and shout, "Stop! Stop! Stop!"

He pulls the whistle, and the train picks up speed. I will jump. I will jump onto the train and find my mother's man and make him come home. My feet hit glass and steel, my knees buckle, I roll down a muddy embankment that smells of raw sewage and oil. In a streak of dizzy light, the train is gone.

I am crying because I can't stand and run after it. My feet are gashed, my knee is swollen, but what impales me to the muddy earth is the sensation of fate ripping life from its bloody pocket and hurling it through me like a comet. I didn't even know I was pregnant. No one ever told me how it happened or how to stop it. And later, after the fetus passes, after the passing too of pain and terror, I remain pinned to the muddy field by my own rage and self-loathing. I damn my mother to hell. And when I'm able to get to my feet, I vow to keep moving.

My mother's grip now has grown raw and strong. Although I would like to stand up, walk to the window and see the train's beacon in the pitch night, she holds me fast to the chair. My gaze crawls over her shrunken eyes and the thick creases and lines of her ancient face, which, like a map, directs me back to my own aching.

Her breath, shallow and sweet with decay, finds a new rhythm as she discovers how to let go of the pain. Her life runs through me. I am filled with her life; I am electric with it.

APPARITIONS

Pallagia felt the shuffle of people in her feet. There would only be a moment of anxiety. A sharp rush, chopping her in two, before the suction would collect her and hurl her into the frenetic scent of touching bodies. Then her vision would return. She would see shadows, turning dark and light in the flickering window frames, and a man with thinning hair, swaying before her, his legs relaxed apart, slowly probing her face with eyes like needles.

When she had first arrived in Montreal she experienced this shameless desire of invasion. On street corners she had looked down, hurried away, whenever searching eyes assaulted, until she developed a taste for it herself. Now she whetted her appetite, letting her eyes travel the length of this passenger in return.

Although difficult to discern, she could tell his sharp face was not like Henri's. His body, perhaps more like Henri's, but old. It was strange the way she had come to measure all men.

She followed the passenger out into the coolness of the platform. Being back here again, she felt in a foreign land, her body recalling the terror of those first days alone, concealing her dark, wavy hair under a black fringed babushka, staring at unaffordable food in shop windows in an effort to hide her face. A face as young and fresh and white as any Easter lily. A face she cursed but eventually found could command a price.

Back in Pallagia's village, her mother had wept over her beauty. "What woman will ever hire you on to keep her house? And how can I ever let you go to a drunken widower?"

Pallagia had learned that beauty was the privilege of the wealthy. It did not assist in the fields, nor could beauty alone attract a good husband. And when for the eldest sister plans of marriage were dashed because of the family's poverty, and employment came to her as housekeeper for the priest, Pallagia, the second eldest, decided she must also seek out her fortune, instead of passively relying on convention.

She worked for a year as a servant, cooking, cleaning and pulling a plow for a neighbouring family who were better off financially than her own but in need of help. The woman of the family was so burdened with children and pregnancy that Pallagia's beauty was of little consequence. All Pallagia asked in return for a year's labour was a ticket that would get her to Canada. Again, her mother wept when she learned of Pallagia's intentions. "Have we made such a bad life for her here?" she asked the priest. Sometimes, still, Pallagia heard her mother weeping.

When Pallagia's eyes dimmed again, Henri stood before her, just as he'd been in those early days, when both their former lives slipped into history. He smelled of coconut, the flavour of his skin. His arms opened like pearled gates to collect her. They would talk like sisters. He would kiss that small space behind her ear where she thoughtfully rested three fingers. He would lie beside her in an ocean of foaming sheets, never caring that she had slept with two thousand men, that the ground around them was muddy with boot marks. He would cradle her cheek to his breast. After they beat her, and took for free what she'd learned to sell, he was the one to find her. Around his head and hands, she recalled, there appeared an ethereal glow. She thought he'd been sent from heaven. A pin of desire scratched her numb heart for his beauty. He carried her so gently, this man with the fiery light, this angel man. He breathed into her a sweet breath. He placed her on a stained mattress in his room. There were no pictures on the walls, no other furniture, only his mattress and a light bulb that swung from the ceiling. He daubed her mouth and eyes with a greying cloth, then rinsed it in a chipped basin. Pallagia watched his burning hands touch the water. A tiny red bud of her blood opened like a crimson rose. His fingers pushed the dark strands of hair away from her face, out of her wounds. Her flesh could have toughened. She could have become stone. But he appeared and she grew strong without hate.

He held her face in his fiery hands when she screamed in the darkness. He held it firmly, as if she were in danger of losing her head. Still, her mother came to her in sleep. She wore a woolen veil over her face and a black shroud on her body. Pallagia searched in vain to see her grey eyes. "You think I wear this veil in mourning, but I wear it out of shame for you."

There had been a riot in the village. The second-youngest daughter, Irina, had been dragged from the house by a soldier. He wound her thick braid around his arm like a rope tied to a mare. He jerked her across the dirt floor as she struggled. The only weapons Pallagia's mother could find were an old broom and a rusted pair of shears. She hit the soldier in the stomach with the broom handle. She forced the rusty shears into his back, where they quivered like a divining rod before he collapsed. When he was dead she put one foot on his back and yanked the shears out. She turned him over to spit in his face and felt a numbness in her left arm, then the explosion of pain in her chest. The soldier was a neighbour's boy. He had lived with them once when his own ill mother could not care for him.

The nightmares began long before the hysterical letters arrived: "Mother is dead. All the fowl slaughtered. The house burned down. Katrina tried to hide the priest under bedclothes, but the soldiers came with swords at the end of their guns. There was blood and goose feathers everywhere. And little Sonia stood watching. She has not spoken since. And how the priest screamed, Pallagia. How he screamed."

Back in her village, Pallagia had slept head to foot with her three sisters, all on one down mattress. She had never grown accustomed to sleeping alone. She woke trembling, crying for them. The letters only made it worse. In time, she became thankful to strangers who bought her for the entire night, no matter how old and unappealing they were. No matter how unshaven and stubbly, and reeking of whiskey and body odour. She opened her arms to them all, embracing them with gratitude. And as for the money, it was faithfully tucked into small envelopes. She did not trust banks. And sister by sister she vowed she would bring them all to her.

Henri advised her to open her own brothel in Windsor, Ontario. He'd once passed through that place, finding it grey, inhospitable, and very much in need of a good house. Only a small river stood between it and Detroit, and so there might be lots of Americans, who spent more freely and made a great show of their wealth.

She found just the house on Drouillard Road. A big firm one with five bedrooms and green wooden siding, and a balcony above, where her girls would sit and smoke cigarettes on cool quiet evenings. She pried open all her little envelopes and paid cash for the house. She bought train tickets for three clean strong beauties from Montreal, and Henri, of course. And the house, as predicted, did well.

There was a steady number of Americans, mostly travelling businessmen, and a regular number of locals, whom Pallagia came to know.

Just down the road was a forty-five-year-old bachelor. A nice quiet man, who owned a house and business of his own, but for all his success had to confess one evening while lying in Pallagia's pale arms that he was a very lonely man.

"You would like my sister, Irina," she told him. "I will be bringing her to Canada soon, and I'm sure she could come all the faster if she had a husband waiting."

She wasted no time in writing to Irina with her happy news: "I have met a kind, wealthy gentleman who would like you as his bride." And in a month, Irina arrived in Canada and at sixteen became a married woman.

Henri held Pallagia on the bed and waited for her to stop shaking. There was a veil of sweat coating her face, and her eyes were cavernous and unseeing.

Just moments before, her mother had stood inches from her, engulfed in flames, shaking a bloody pair of shears.

"This is what I killed for? This is what I died for? I would rather kill you." Her words had no edge. They rolled off her tongue.

Henri peeled the damp sheet off Pallagia's naked body. Her flesh felt clammy rather than hot. He lay washcloths of ice water over her wrists and ankles, across her forehead. He sent one of the others to summon the doctor—a trustworthy man, a regular client, who prescribed antibiotics for the clap, and helped the girls out of unfortunate situations.

Henri told Pallagia afterwards how she'd pleaded with him to put her clothes on so her mother would not be ashamed, how the doctor had come and examined her, and the house had been discreetly locked up.

What the illness was the doctor couldn't say, but the fever was so high that, even with antibiotics, he could not be hopeful. For seventy-two hours, Henri held her when she could stand it, or kneeled at the foot of her bed when she could not. He propped her head and dribbled water through her parched blistering lips. No one else came near.

He never once believed she would die, even when the doctor told him to call the priest. And after seventy-two hours, the worst had ended.

When she was strong again, she sent for her sister Sonia, who was only thirteen, and stuttered when she tried to speak. "But there is such a husband here for you, my dear little Sonia," Pallagia wrote her. "He is an excellent doctor. A kind, lonely man who will treat you like a princess."

Sonia arrived in a mist. Her dark eyes looked like empty saucers. Her body was like a small child's. She clutched Pallagia's sleeve when she was introduced to the old doctor.

"She's starving and has ringworm, and she might even be brain damaged. What kind of wife is this?"

He was indignant, but Pallagia calmed him. "You are a great doctor," she told him. "Just think how you will own her if you make her well. And she is pretty. Even sick, she is pretty."

The doctor looked at her large black eyes and her pale skin. There was a certain ghoulish beauty about her. He took her home, but made no promises. And when he came for his weekly visits to the brothel, he was full of complaints about her. "She collects food from the pantry and hides it under the bed. I've seen her eat beetles off the window ledge....Revolting! Holding her is like wrestling a sack of bones."

But Pallagia knew her sister kept the doctor's house clean and neat, and already, under his care, was beginning to develop breasts and hips and beginning to look like a woman. "Oh yes," Pallagia had said to him, "but I know one or two men who would pay to hold a little virgin like my sister." That was enough to stop the doctor's complaints. Sonia blossomed into a voluptuous flower, and her reticence in the old man's bed only increased her desirability.

Although he still came to the brothel, he came less and less, as Pallagia would never fail to point out. "My sister does very well for you?" she'd ask contritely. And the doctor would grin.

But then, there was the question of Katrina. And for all her jovial ways with the customers, Pallagia couldn't hide her distress from Henri.

"She is twenty-one next birthday, and although pretty in her own way, not a real beauty. What man will I find for her? What if she arrives sick like Sonia?"

For nights, Pallagia couldn't sleep. Figures ran through her head, decimal points and zeros. Every now and again, she would turn, startled to catch a glimpse of her mother, creeping across a wall, camouflaged in shadow. "She will never forgive me, never." Pallagia wept, falling to her knees.

Henri lifted her into his arms. "You are forgiven," he

told her, and his voice sounded like an angel's. He
kissed her on the forehead with his open mouth. He
tucked her into bed, gave her morphia, and lay beside
her until she slept.

He made inquires at the bar. Did any man there need
a good wife?

"And who do you have in mind?" asked an acquain-
tance. "Whores make terrible wives."

He swallowed a mouthful of beer. "Not a whore, a
decent girl, Pallagia's sister."

"But Pallagia's sister has married the doctor. Don't
tell me he doesn't want her now?"

And several men laughed at this, and laughed again
when they heard Pallagia had yet another sister named
Katrina.

"Is she as lithe in bed?" asked one man.

"Is she as beautiful?" asked another.

Henri told Pallagia all this the following day when
they sat together at breakfast. And then, it was a miracle.
A stranger—a northern man—came into the bar. He said
he would take Katrina unseen. Pallagia kissed Henri a
hundred times and immediately sent a letter to her eldest
sister: "God has provided you with a husband here, who,
although not wealthy, is intelligent and well-travelled."

Katrina arrived from a refugee camp with her head
cast down. She carried a small straw basket, no longer
tightly woven, containing all her possessions. Sonia's
doctor treated her for dysentery and anemia and she
was married to the northern stranger, who seemed
accepting of her appearance.

"Now all your sisters are here and secure, you should sleep better," Henri told Pallagia, wrapping his happy arms under hers, and kissing her long, slender neck. And it was true that the dreams and visions of her mother no longer plagued her as they once had done. But now, her sleeps were restless because she was forbidden to see her sisters. She was a whore. No decent woman would have anything to do with her. And when Irina had a daughter, and when that daughter had grown old enough to know better than to stop at the corner of Drouillard Road and speak to Auntie Pallagia, it felt as if Pallagia's heart had been torn out and trampled.

"But your father comes to my house!" she told her niece. "I always send him home at supper time! Your mother—my sister—is a wealthy woman. She has everything she could ever wish for. Why does she begrudge me my conversations with my little niece?"

And the niece would run past as if Pallagia were some crazy witch.

One ferocious winter, long after Pallagia had grown too old for whoring and after the police finally closed her house down, Henri crawled into her bed and embraced her. His body was cold and wrinkled and they clung to one another as if shipwrecked.

He died in her arms, and she took him back to Montreal to be buried there. It was a different city than the place they had met. But in her ninetieth year, on the night of her return, Henri came to her, promising to take her to heaven.

PASSION IN REMISSION

They carried him out of the house on one of our kitchen chairs. He was that skinny and weak, he couldn't walk, but I thought he was just being theatrical.

They were taking him to court. Our dog got out of the yard, pissed all over the neighbour's shrubs, and killed them.

I held the door and watched him hunch on the chair. He was hanging onto the seat with both hands. His knuckles were almond-coloured with effort.

The seat and back of the chair used to be red vinyl and smelled of new dolls. Then mom read in one of her magazines about making old furniture new again, and re-upholstered the whole set with scratchy brown fabric she picked up at K-mart on the clearance table along with a bunch of big golden tacks.

Could have been the very chair he'd hurled in the air the night the astronauts landed on the moon. I looked carefully to see if the back was crooked or if there were any tacks missing.

If it was the chair, mom sure had done a good job of putting it back together again. No one ever would have known. She re-upholstered two living room chairs too and started the ruffle of the couch. Then, she ran out of steam for re-upholstering and started antiquing everything. Black and red, gold and white, black and green, black and blue. For months, I stuck to everything I touched, and that singeing smell of paint made my head ache.

I didn't think he had a chance in hell of winning. I watched him down the concrete porch steps. His face was like an imploded prune. Well, maybe they'd feel sorry for him.

None of us were going to court with him. It was something he wanted to do alone, though I found out later we were probably the only ones in the whole neighbourhood who didn't attend. Mrs. Bazos, the Hungarian woman at the end of our street who talked like Zsa Zsa Gabor, said she told the judge, "Why don't you leave this poor man alone, can't you see he's sick?"

I imagined him on the witness stand. I imagined him stamping his foot and pounding his fist. I imagined him saying, "So what if it was a white dog, three foot high on all fours, so what .... Maybe it was someone else's dog. How can you be so certain it was my dog?"

He could work himself up into a passion when he wanted to. He could make his voice go high and desperate. There was that time when he was jumping up and down in this department store after my brother had been caught shoplifting. "Let me see my son! Take me to my son!" People crowded around. The security woman, who was supposed to keep him out front while they pried a confession loose from my brother in the back room, buckled. She was no match at all for him.

"How do you know my son did it?" He was indignant. He howled. Everyone could hear him. Everyone was so quiet. It was like live theatre. It was that wrenching, grieving, horrific note only he could manufacture. He walked out with my brother and drove away. But I thought, no, he could only be pathetic now.

"She took us to court because she's jealous," my mother clucked. She was into ceramics now and had a streak of glaze on her cheek.

We all thought our neighbours coveted our dog. Penny, the neighbour who lost her shrubs, owned a yappy little nothing of a puppy.

We also thought they coveted our pool. Even if it was green most of the time and we couldn't swim in it. We knew he lost that night. He never said anything, but we knew because he didn't tell us he won, and if he had won, he would have wanted to tell us blow by blow how it happened. If he hadn't been so sick, I know he would have been drinking. He would have drunk himself into a snit and maybe thrown another kitchen chair or broken something my mother was making.

He was pretty nasty anyway and had been even before he found out he had cancer and they did the operation. But now he was just lying on the orange couch with the unfinished yellow ruffle, his head tilted back on a cushion, his mouth open like he was having trouble breathing. A fine white powder that looked like dried milk around his lips. His eyes kind of rolling back in his head. I sat looking at him, wondering if he practised that in front of the mirror. It was very convincing. It could tear your heart right out of your chest if you didn't know him. Still, it hadn't done him any good in court.

In the morning, I heard him talking to my grand-mother. She was coming almost every day now, and my mother was getting used to scuttling off to the basement to avoid her.

"Ma, promise me you'll look after the kids," he whined. "Promise me you'll see them through school."

I waited, hearing my heart tick, and the creak of my bed. It was like listening for a car to jump start, or a fur-nace to kick in, or a Christmas cracker to explode. "Come on," I thought, tightening my fists, "come on."

When he'd first wanted to move here and didn't have the money, he'd lit into her then. "We're flesh and blood," he'd said, "These are the only grandchildren you'll ever have. Loan me the money for a house. If pa were alive, he'd give me the money." His eyes flashed with success. His voice rose and crashed and threw her clear off her objections. She handed him a crumpled cheque. One she dug out way at the bottom of her purse. Her hand trembled when she signed it. Her face and lips were so flat and tight you could have served drinks on them. We moved in two weeks later. He was that sure of himself he'd already made a bid and started packing.

Now, there was only silence. She hadn't even responded. She just walked out. Well, Jesus Christ, I thought as the screen door slammed and my father panted. My mother scaled the creaking basement stairs as my grandmother's car pulled away.

"Can I make you a nice piece of sirloin steak?" She asked him in a fake, singsong voice. "How about a chicken sandwich? Spaghetti? Minestrone soup? I can warm up the minestrone soup, no trouble. Beans on toast? Pickles? How about pizza? I can order a pizza."

I was still in my room but imagined him lying out there above the yellow ruffle, moving his shrivelled head slowly to and fro, as if to give it a good decisive shake might damage it. And those vertical pain lines in his face so deep you could hide things in them. I clenched my teeth. Jesus Christ, I thought. Jesus Christ.

"Ice cream," she continued, "a sundae, cashews, fruit, or how about Chinese food? You've always been partial to it. I could phone now, and they'd bring it in a jiff."

"Jesus Christ." It emerged from my mouth this time like torn flesh. "Jesus bloody Christ!" I stood on my bed. My voice sliced the walls, stuck my mother in the throat and continued out past the front door. My hands, fists, rising over my head. Rising to the ceiling.

UGLY HANDS

Myroslav poured sweet raspberry wine into his teacup, wine he had made himself, thick as blood. It hurt his teeth to drink it, yet there was nothing else to take. The wines he favoured had disappeared. The beer, the vodka, the whiskey, all gone too.

Olya made noises like a frightened squirrel. She had been sweeping the floor, pushing, then pulling the broom forcefully. Straw bristles cracked and fell away like the ragged white hairs on the top of her head, and now she stood behind Myroslav, her sharp, grey eyes carving his back.

She regretted leaving her village, running away as she had. Braver hearts had survived and were now rebuilding the country, building better lives, but her life for many years now had been here, far from her family, married to Myroslav, who drank much too much and earned much too little.

"I'm just tasting, Olya," he said night after night, "just making sure it's coming along." But by morning, the bottle was always empty and Myroslav always sleeping on the table, his cheek flush to wood.

Olya knew it could have been worse, she knew of men who turned to devils when they drank, tearing up their homes, beating their wives and children. This was not Myroslav's way. Instead he became silly with her, he teased, he told idiotic stories, and when she rebuked him for his buffoonery, he would become withdrawn and indolent. She saw to it now that all the younger children were fed an early supper of bread and milk and put to bed before he came home, but Nastya, the eldest and her father's favourite, was not so easily closeted.

Some nights before he had grown stupid with alcohol, he spoke to Nastya about politics, his work, trouble on the assembly line, and Olya could not shut him up.

She would become a fiend with her broom, sweeping like a mad woman. "Lift your feet, lift your feet," she'd snap, cracking the broom like a rifle, admonishing her husband and daughter for not wiping their shoes properly as they came in the door.

"Come help me make your father's supper," she'd shout to Nastya, rattling pots and pans and dishes. "Come learn something useful."

And Myroslav would pour another cup of wine, and let his bony backside sink ever deeper into the warm curves of his chair.

Nastya followed her mother into the kitchen where windows dripped with condensation and the smell of cabbage clung to walls. On the stove, broth bubbled furiously. The old black pan lid thumped like a heart.

Olya pushed a bowl of peas across the unsteady table for Nastya to shell. She planned on Nastya being out of the house by Easter. A well-to-do family, friends of the priest, needed a housekeeper. Olya had put a word in for Nastya and was certain the job would come through, although she hadn't mentioned a word of it yet.

Nastya's hands worked quickly over the peas, although they appeared too large and clumsy for the task. They had grown thick and heavy from canning, and gnarled like her mother's.

"Cook and clean, make a decent home, for what?" her mother chanted, and then snapped the bowl away from Nastya. "I could have shelled all of those peas by now."

Myroslav winced as he drank his wine. It was painful to hear his wife's tirades. She picked on Nastya and thought he was a failure. Yet how could she think otherwise when he thought the very same of himself? Hours and years of toil on the line did not bring him a farm. There was bread on the table, a roof over their heads, but this was not enough.

He had bought a second-hand Plymouth from a friend, unseen. A good, inexpensive vehicle to get to and from work and transport his family to church on Sundays. Olya seethed when he told her about it. Bad enough him spending money they didn't have, but buying a used car they didn't need seemed sinful.

"What if you or the children got sick, and the doctor couldn't come?" Myroslav argued. "You'd be happy of a car then."

But Olya only scowled and shrugged. Sometimes Myroslav could not decide what was worse, Olya's tongue striking or relaxing petulantly in silence. Olya refused to be driven anywhere, and Myroslav found it difficult to park, and so, for the most part, the car did not fulfill its destiny, but sat on a yellow patch of grass in the front yard shaded by fruit trees.

"It will rust after winter," Olya said. Her prophecies carried the power of curses, and Myroslav shuddered when he heard them.

Myroslav's neighbours, fellows he worked with, chided him about the way he feared her. But none of them could really find fault with her. She kept a tidy house and was a decent cook. She planted and tended Myroslav's garden, sold fresh fruit and vegetables at the market. She milked his goat, and raised his children to be clean and respectful. At church, she was highly thought of. She baked pies and on occasion did house-keeping for the priest. Myroslav's friends and neighbours all agreed among themselves it was he who needed reform and spoke to him often. If only he could show more strength in his marriage. It was no good for any-one if a wife was allowed to dominate. Other wives would become uncertain and discontented. It seemed to Myroslav's friends it was his duty, not only as head of his family but as a member of the community, to take a stronger stand.

"Don't you have enough troubles of your own?" he'd ask the men who spoke so seriously to him. "I just want a peaceful life." And, in this way, he would put a momentary end to their sermons, and they would drink a glass of wine or whiskey with him and turn their attentions to problems at work.

Just last week, Sasha Duborik was found in a ditch with his throat slit open like a plum. Two weeks before, it was Vladimir Dempsky. The word "union" was like a poison kiss for any man who dared to hold it on his lips. The men's widows were left destitute, their orphaned children homeless, and no one could do anything to assist these unfortunate families. Even the funerals could not be attended, flowers could not be sent, grief could not be openly felt without the risk of endangering one's own family.

Myroslav let the sweet alcohol roll in his mouth as he contemplated. He was not a man at all like Duborik or Dempsky. Perhaps he wasn't as stupid, or perhaps not quite as wise, but he found no glory in battle.

He thought of his own little family: Olya, who in spite of her temper was a devoted mother and wife, and the younger children, who were growing up like strong trees, and then, of course, his own Nastya, whose company he enjoyed more than any. How could a man risk the welfare of his family for some elusive goal? The idea was absurd to him. He was an easily contented man, willing to take whatever was offered. He was happy to be alive and free, to be fed and clothed and housed and, yes, even to be drunk.

He raised his teacup toward the kitchen in a mock toast as Nastya arrived to tell him dinner was ready, and suddenly shrouded in the radiant warmth of wine he blurted that Nastya must have driving lessons, that he would teach her himself in the old Plymouth. That, indeed, there was no reason for her not to learn.

Olya dropped a plate. Boiled potatoes rolled into the far corners of the kitchen, and Nastya quickly moved with her apron to retrieve them.

"Look what you've made me do, you foolish man," Olya shouted, "talking such stupidity."

But Myroslav did not take it back. "We have a car," he said, "and what if an emergency should arise one day, what if I should fall ill, if I should have a heart attack. It makes perfectly good sense." His words joined like a knitted chain, and he struggled to sound sober.

"It makes no sense!" Olya bellowed, "You make no sense! Put your bottle away. Come eat your dinner."

But even as he ate, Myroslav continued defending his enthusiasm, as Olya worked equally to ignore it. "Why shouldn't Nastya drive? Why shouldn't she? I tell you it is the most sensible thing."

Nastya sat quietly looking at her plate as her father rambled and poured himself another cup of wine. She felt the silent vice-like pressure her mother exerted closing in around her, but she struggled not to say a word. If her father would have her drive, she would not go against him.

Later that evening, as she washed the dishes and wiped down the stove and table, her mother angrily whispered that she should have refused her father's plan. "By saying nothing, you encourage him in it," Olya admonished, "and what do you think other people will have to say about it?" Olya cracked her dishtowel with rage; yet Myroslov went ahead with his plans.

It became a habit after work, before he was too drunk to see, for Myroslav to set up a dozen bushel baskets for Nastya to manoeuvre around. Sometimes she would hit one and make it splinter or skid into the raspberry bushes, but before long she twisted the wheel of the car with such dexterity, it was almost as if it had become a part of her.

"You're a better driver than me!" Myroslav crowed, slapping his thick calloused hand over his daughter's shoulder. Now that she had gained confidence he was eager to take her out onto the streets where it would be easier to display and boast about her accomplishments.

He told every man he knew about his great success in teaching his daughter to drive. The more he drank, it seemed, the more he enjoyed bragging, but the men he told did not share his enthusiasm.

"It's like teaching fish to fly," one neighbour said, "wrong, unnatural."

And many others lamented the fact that now he had taught his daughter to drive, other wives and daughters might think they too should be taught.

"Think, Myroslav, of the trouble you cause us," Olya said, after finding former friends turn cold. "I forbid you to make any of our children into trick monkeys."

But Myroslav had made the decision not to back down to Olya, to be firm in this. So what if a few old birds got their feathers ruffled? His Nastya could drive that old Plymouth better than he himself could. Now that was something to drink to and he did, and tomorrow after work he would drink to it again. He would buy a round of drinks at the public house and have Nastya wait for him outside in the car. It would be worth the money it cost him to see the expression on the faces of his astonished neighbours as Nastya drove them both away.

It was a thought, a vision that provided such pleasure, his mind would not let go of it. And when the following evening arrived, after Myroslav had dragged his tired body home from work and drained one of the younger smaller bottles of wine, he called his daughter from the kitchen, and he laughed and hugged her and told her that she made him very proud.

It was a frosty evening, and the moon sat luminous in the clear, star-filled sky. Nastya started the car, and Myroslav wiped steam from the windows. As they pulled away, both could see Olya's plaintive face. She was standing on the concrete porch, clutching her ragged sweater to her chest.

They drove wordlessly down darkened roads where thin beams of light appeared through the shadows, and trees seemed animate and bowed toward them. "Keep your eyes focused," Myroslav directed, for he knew how strange lights played tricks with the eyes, and Nastya absorbed his comment and continued driving, her silent face smoother than rock.

Just beyond a small bend that curved in a fork toward town, where withered cornfields merged in hazy light, Myroslav was aware of sudden movement, a deer or pheasant perhaps. He forced his eyes forward, away from distraction, but Nastya, seeing more clearly the movement, brought the car to a halt.

Six men encircled the old black car. Their faces were hidden, but the stance of their bodies was familiar to Myroslav. Something shone like glistening silver in their hands, and they moved in a slow, circular dance, surrounding the car, as if it were a wild animal and they anxious hunters.

In the morning, Olya awoke alone in her bed, trembling with grief and panic as factory whistles called workers to life.

TROPHIES

A dusty five-by-seven photograph of my father dressed in khaki, his hand extended above his brow touching the end of his garrison cap in mock salute, graces the top of the television set he gave my grandmother. It sits right next to the dark brown rabbit ears antenna he spends hours fiddling with in the sweltering summer heat, while she perches on the chesterfield, advising him in a language I don't understand.

I dance around him, my excited limbs impatient and electric for the opportunity to swim. Grandma lives in a house close to Lake Erie. It's a house he helped build, with a blue-shingled roof and a powder-blue concrete porch, and every summer he brings us here.

Outside, there is an acre of fruit trees: nectarine, plum, pear, cherry, a variety of apple, and nut. There are berries of all kinds, and a white ceramic birdbath in the front yard, which collects falling leaves that turn the water vermilion.

My mother sits tensely at my grandmother's kitchen

table, smoking cigarettes, drumming her fingers on the plastic-covered tablecloth. My grandmother lifts herself from the couch and tells me to follow her. The air is stale in her shadowy bedroom where she offers me a chocolate cherry from a black vinyl handbag.

She retrieves a piece of newspaper from a carved teak box on her night table and pushes it into my hand. "When he come back from Korea, he going to be marry nice Ukrainian girl," she says in a low conspiratorial whisper. "Since they being children, they going to be marry."

I look at the clipping. It is an engagement announcement, and a photograph of my father with his arm around a smiling fair-haired woman. "Your mamma being no good," she tells me emphatically, and gives me another chocolate cherry and a five-dollar bill.

When my father has fixed the picture on my grandmother's set, my mother tosses her pearly-buttoned white angora sweater over her shoulders and hurries outside across my grandmother's lawn to the car. The heels of her patent-leather sling-backs sink in the mud as she passes the squishy grass around the birdbath. For a moment, she struggles to release herself, as if she has fallen into a trap, but recovers and is first in the car. Ten minutes away, down a chalky dirt road, in a wood-frame cottage, lives a girl my age named Jo. She's the daughter of an old friend of my mother's. The fact her family chose to settle here strikes everyone as an amazing coincidence—except my mother, who sees it as a blessing.

Jo's parents, Mary and Nat, wait on their porch in faded lawn chairs, drinking beer, and jump up fast when we pull over the bit of gravel that is their drive-way. Mary, in square dark glasses and a striped strapless shell and shorts, embraces my mother, while Nat grins and taps my father on the arm. Jo appears from behind the house. She's shy but shares my enthusiasm for swimming, and we run down the rickety stairs behind their property and wade into the lake. It is dusk before we return. Our mothers nurse gin and tonics, smoke cigarettes and swat at mosquitoes, while we rub our-selves on beach towels, letting pounds of sand drop out of our suits onto the patchy lawn.

Mary met my mother when they were girls in England. She was bridesmaid at my parents' wedding, and the only friend my mother trusted enough to tell she was three months' pregnant when she got married.

My mother looks past me. "To tell the truth," she says, her words slightly slurred, "I did it on purpose. I was afraid he'd go back to her."

Inside, my father and Nat are gulping beer and mak-ing pancakes. My father knows how to flip them three feet in the air, which impresses both Nat and Jo. I know he learned how to do this in Korea, and when the plate of pancakes is ready and sitting before us, I ask my father to tell a war story.

He sits crossed-legged on the floor, Nat laughs and says, "Two beers for two queers," and pushes my father another bottle. When Jo asks my father what he did in the war, he says he was a stamp collector.

Sometimes he tells true stories about flaming jellied gasoline, and about crippled orphaned children begging for rations, but he never tells the truth anymore about being a soldier.

Today he eats his pancakes and drinks his beer in silence. When we finish, he and Nat make Jo and me go outside to play.

We chase fireflies that alight on the lower leaves of wild rose bushes and catch them in our cupped hands. When we have caught a dozen, we let them go. They flicker like tiny moving stars, forming a fleeting constellation all in one moment.

We leave at midnight. My father is so drunk he drives on the highway slower than I can walk. His car zigzags sluggishly from one lane to another. My mother talks to him in a soft voice, artificially calm. She asks if he'd rather pull over for a rest, find coffee, or go back and stay the night. My father swears, accelerates and swerves. I hold my breath and half close my eyes until the headlights on the highway are a blur. The following morning, I wake in my own bed.

The fine velvet smoking jacket that smells both sweet and spicy hangs at the back of my father's closet. He wears it more often now he's drinking again. His trim brown hair sticks out in places; he discards his black framed glasses. He is beginning to look like a stranger.

My mother tells me some Korean woman gave him the jacket, and later, when I'm looking through my father's wooden desk for a piece of paper, a picture of her slides out of a brown manila envelope. Her name,

Yoko, has been penned on the back in my father's precise angular handwriting. She is slender and exotic, her cheekbones high, her waist-length hair is thick and black. Inside the envelope there are more photographs of her. In some, she is naked.

Her breasts are pointed, the nipples dark, her pubic area a perfect triangle of black. The expression on her face is weary. There is also a bundle of her personal letters, written partly in English. They all begin, "My dearest husband," and end, "your loving wife." I tuck it all neatly back into the envelope and shut the desk drawer, erasing everything.

My father brings my mother a box of long-stemmed burgundy roses. They perfume the air, even before they are lifted out. He fetches a glass vase from her china cabinet and places them prominently in the centre of the dining room table. When my mother sees them, she begins to cry. Her hand moves toward her heart, then in a spasm, jumps forward, smashing the vase to crystal wedges, crippling the flowers. "Give them to your lover," she shouts.

At night, my parents argue. My mother threatens, then destroys the good set of dishes and the porcelain knick-knacks she's painstakingly collected. Through a crack in my bedroom door, I see my father collapse over the kitchen sink, sobbing. In the morning my mother packs a mottled ivory suitcase. She says she is going to England. She drops a white-gloved hand that smells of peppermint gum on my shoulder, and tells me when I'm a little older, I can take a plane by myself across the ocean. She kisses me on the forehead before her taxi arrives. I let the red stain of her lipstick stay there long after she's gone.

My father and I drive to my grandmother's house. She greets us both with kisses, and pinches my cheeks hard between her thumbs and forefingers. She ushers us into her house, calls me into her bedroom, and presents me with an impressive box of chocolate cherries and a hundred-dollar savings bond. She says nothing about my mother.

My father fiddles with the rabbit ears, fixes the picture on her set. In the late afternoon, he asks if I would like to go for a swim.

The air is hot and humid. The hazy sun hides behind turgid clouds. We drive for ten minutes down Jo's familiar dusty road, and then my father tells me, Mary has left Nat.

We pull into their makeshift driveway. Everything looks decayed. Beer cans and a rusty barbeque litter the front lawn. An old bicycle with broken spokes leans against a grey sagging fence. The cottage itself, with its concave roof, looks like a warped crate.

Jo's bloodless face appears through the living room window. Her eyes are as large and empty as clamshells. She watches my father collect a square bag from the trunk of his car and carry it into the cottage. He presents us both with a red stamp album, already with several colourful Oriental stamps inside, and warns us to take care of these. Now it's time to swim, he tells us.

We leave the house and make our way to the churning

water. The wind ties our hair in knots that lash our faces. Dead carp, condoms, and a toilet seat buffet the shore. We wade up to our knees in the sticky water and stand there, motionless, unable to go any farther.

Black clouds eat the sky, rolling in faster than muddy waves. A fork of lightning spears the lake with an explosion. We run back, flying over broken stairs, the white flash still searing.

We do not stop to dry the sand off our legs but enter the calm darkened cottage. There is a day-old newspaper crumpled in the corner of the living room, two beers abandoned by our fathers sit on the chipped wooden coffee table. Someplace, in a back bedroom there is a groan.

FLYING HORSES

I hear the toilet flush and know it's midnight; his feet march over bathroom tiles. In fifteen minutes, the splintering porch door will open, then shut. He'll head for the living room, stand at a window, peek out through dented blinds, stiff as an ancient ghost.

I hold my breath listening, wondering, though I know what should happen next. I should hear mom, her pink fluffy slippers like powder puffs dusting the hall.

"Come back to bed." That's what she tells him. Her voice is always gentle. I'm resting on my elbows, the muscles in my body tighter than a stretched cable. I think of my sister across the hall, wonder if she's sleeping. I send her telepathic messages.

"How's it going?" I ask her, "You awake?" I try to sound calm, friendly.

I imagine her in the darkness, small as a bug in the centre of her bed, thinking back to me, "I'm OK," or dreaming of magic castles and flying horses that take her right outside the house and up into the air.

When she was younger, you couldn't shut her up about flying horses. She saw them everywhere. In the clouds, on streets, in stores. Mostly they hid in our basement or under our parents' bed. They thought someone was going to shoot them. They waited till everyone was sleeping, then nudged themselves free, clip-clopped down the hallway, stood outside her bedroom. She wanted to go with them, but was afraid they might not bring her back, afraid she might slip from their silvery magic, fall just before she reached the moon. She'd cry about it in the mornings. Then she'd piss herself. "If I don't go with them, they'll leave and never come back," she'd howl. Mom tried to comfort her. She tried to pretend it was the most natural thing in the world.

"Lots of kids have imaginary friends," she told my sister's teacher. The teacher showed her all the pictures my sister drew. Horses and people. Our entire family, hacked apart. Mom brought the pictures home, then she took us out of school, moved us all the way out here to the country, said her kids didn't need a shrink, and that she could teach us better anyway.

The flying horses left. They blinked their big bashful eyes, waved their hooves and flew. "They were scared," my sister whispered, "they couldn't live with us anymore." That was the last she said about them.

Mom taught us at the kitchen table every night after work, and he didn't mind so much as long as we were quiet. She picked up old math texts and readers and made us learn. Neither of us cared for school, and it was fun in the day to bike all the way into town, look in the stores, drop by the restaurant for free pop and watch mom work. Then her boss said we couldn't hang around, so we rode our bikes in the opposite direction, way, way out past the fields. We climbed trees, sometimes picked apples and berries and Indian corn, made cigarettes from dried leaves.

We tried to stay out in the fields as long as we could, watching the pink sun fall behind trees, talking about what we'd do when we were old enough to decide. We didn't want to go home and bother him, but then he said it was dangerous in the fields: "Hell, could be land mines out there." My sister wet herself, mom made us stay inside. That was two months ago.

I've learned how to get out of my bed without making a sound, tiptoe invisibly through the house. I know what to do, how to cover my face with a wet cloth, hold my breath without panicking. I know how to hide, I know how to crawl on my belly like a snake, how not to get hit by a shell, how to take the things I need. I know what it means to survive. I know there are things you never say, things you never do, and then there are things you always do, even when they seem unimportant; even when you're too tired, you do them anyway.

I've learned how to put my ear against doors without touching them, how to sniff out the different members of my family five hundred yards away. French fries and cigarette smoke is mom, even after a shower. Molly always smells of piss. But his smell clings everywhere, even to mom and Molly sometimes. It holds like heavy tar, seeps in through the cracks, wherever he stands, wherever he moves.

He guards the windows, monitors the doors, every half-hour he makes the rounds. There are vents big enough to house bombs, locks weak enough to smash with one strong hammering. He's installing extra dead-bolts, extra chains, pulling wire as thin as guitar string around and through every piece of furniture, every ornament, every handle, every latch. Sometimes the explosions rattle the house. Sometimes the flashes burn into you, the sounds deaden you; it can take hours before you realize it's over, that you got through it, and then without warning it can start all over again.

He knows about guerilla war tactics, he's read *The Art of War*, done time in the jungle, danced on the skulls of weaker or braver men. He used to tell stories all the time. He used to wave his fist in the air, bring it down hard, break things with it. Mom told us just ignore it, just nod, so we did, then he'd tell us more.

It got so we were dreaming about it every night. About machine gun holes like red pinpricks in the chest that take your entire back off, splatter your yellow guts on the ceiling; about arms and legs and hands that go missing after a flash of hot light; and fountains of blood that shoot into the air across a room.

"You're lucky," he told us, "goddamned lucky that I made it through, that I'm here now, that I can protect you."

When the noise comes, he shifts toward the Venetian blinds, stands well to the side, dips an aluminum slat with his baby finger, then pivots, kicking the front door wide, and starts firing.

Molly and I drop under the kitchen table, we hold each other like babies while he's yelling at us to take cover in our rooms. I try to pull Molly, make her crawl upstairs with me, but her eyes are like stone and I know she isn't hearing. "Please, just don't piss yourself," I beg her, knowing that this is ridiculous, it shouldn't matter.

Clouds of choking smoke and a hail of sharp debris twist over us. I yank Molly by the arm and she screams.

"Get the hell out of here, now!" he shouts above the deafening blasts, and I pull Molly up the stairs, even though she resists, even though her arm cracks and she's crying and shouting for me to stop.

After the skirmish, he lectures us: "If I tell you to move, you move. If I tell you stay, you stay. If I tell you to shit, you shit. Do you understand? You don't ask questions. You just follow orders."

Molly shivers in her wet pants, cradles her injured arm. We both stand attentively, nod our heads emphatically. He disappears to make his next round.

Mom gives Molly a bath, puts a sling around her arm, makes supper. We sit at the table, ignoring the wires that run between and around us.

"You should have seen the bastards run," he's telling her, beer foam collecting in the corners of his mouth. "I set some more traps this afternoon. So much for the enemy. Those bastards won't get in... at least not in one piece!"

He tells us all he's got a new plan. He hands out a different map. Everywhere an X appears, he's buried explosives. There are some now in the flower beds, in the window boxes, all around my sister's playhouse outside, a whole new system strategically located in the basement.

"When the war's over," mom whispers to Molly, "you'll be able to play outside again."

I notice mom across the table, giving me the kind of hard look she gives when she wants me to shut up.

"I didn't say anything," I tell her, and she turns away from me like she doesn't hear.

"When will the war be over?" Molly asks. She's sobbing, clinging to the sleeve of mom's dress, pulling at it like her fingers can't let go. "Please make it stop!" Her eyes are scared wild. She looks like someone who can't breathe. Like someone who's slowly bleeding to death.

Mom tries to loosen her fingers. She looks into her eyes, speaks very slowly. "When the war ends you can go back to school. I'll buy you pretty dresses. You can ride your bike out into the field and not be afraid anymore."

He throws some kind of hand grenade. A huge white streak sucks the air dry, an explosion louder than any I've ever heard shakes the house and makes it sound as if it's cracking into tiny pieces. Stone, dirt and gravel shower the roof like broken stars.

"Take cover," he yells, smashing a board off the living room window with his rifle, but all of us are already under something solid and lying flush to the ground.

I smell Molly's pee and think I'm going to be sick. "Get to your rooms! You know the drill!" He's shouting. The shrubs at the front of the house are flaming like bonfires. "Move it!" he orders.

Mom strokes Molly's hair, lifts her to her feet. A second explosion turns the world orange, everything suddenly goes dull.

"When the war's over," I hear my mother murmur to Molly as she rocks her back and forth, "When it's over. When it's over."

It's a broken record, a nightmare, my ears are thumping like jack hammers and I don't know if I'm really hearing it or not. "Shut the fuck up!" I tell her. "Get to your rooms!" I hunt around with my hands in the chalky clouds of plaster for a rifle.

Smoke and dust roll like a warm wave through the house. Broken plaster, splinters of wood, shattered glass, sprinkle us from the air.

"Make the war stop!" Molly shouts. She's looking at me now, asking me to end it. If I could find a goddamned rifle, maybe I could do something, or at least try.

"Get to your room, Molly," I order. She stands there, waiting. She stands there, while the whole fucking world burns, while bullets rip into walls and smoke as thick as meat pours into our lungs.

Mom tries to move her. "Help me," she chokes, struggling to lift Molly into her arms. The smell of piss is overwhelming.

"I can't," I say.

"Do what I tell you!" my mother shouts, and I come close to helping, but when I touch Molly's wet pants, I start gagging and give up.

I surrender deliberately, loudly, so Molly can hear me above the din of gunfire and the crash of breaking earth outside. "There is no war." Mom furrows her brows, shoots poison from her eyes at me.

Molly's eyes are wider than moons. Mom goes to cover Molly's ears.

"You wanted me to help," I say, but suddenly she's strong enough to get Molly up the stairs on her own, strong enough to turn her back on me.

"Fuckin' cowards," he's shouting through broken boards, "Come out and fight, you yellow bastards!"

I stand watching mom go, Molly coughing and crying, smoke rolling over us like black film.

GRAINS OF SALT

We stood in a semicircle watching mom come through the door. She was carrying that little square vinyl bag she used to use for selling cosmetics. One of the straps got broken a long time ago, and she'd bleached out the golden *V* in the bottom left-hand corner, but, still, every time I saw that bag, I could hear the jingle of a dozen white-capped bottles and see a rainbow of miniature lipsticks.

I remember sometimes after dad went to bed, she'd wake me up, even though I had school in the morning, and we'd sit together at the kitchen table painting each other's fingernails and toenails with Primrose Pink or Luscious Lemon Berry, while she gossiped over customers and talked about the future.

She told me she would become rich selling cosmetics. That she would buy an in-the-ground swimming pool and take us all on a world cruise. When she changed her mind and gave up selling, I didn't leave my room for a week. But then I got bored with being mad and

disappointed, and my dad said if I ever hoped to survive in the world, I was going to have to learn how to
take people like my mother with a grain of salt, so I got
over it.

Her hair was pulled back now in a neat tight bun, and
she didn't have a speck of colour, real or artificial, on
her face. It was déjà vu, except the last time it happened
she was cradling a yellow baby shawl with her free arm,
and my little brother, Derek, newborn and sleepy, was
tucked inside. That arm, the one that should have been
holding him, hung with a palm out-turned. And we all
pretended not to notice when she tripped a little bit over
the weather-stripping at the threshold, and her feet
pulled across the parquet floor.

Dad stood behind, guiding her with a soft hand. He
was a good six inches shorter than her, and at least two
times as fat and sometimes seeing them together made
me want to laugh, but in the end I'd feel so bad, I didn't.

I looked into my mother's face—into her green-grey
eyes, which we had determined together one night were
exactly the same shade as mine, but I saw nothing familiar. Her pupils were like the heads of burnt-out match-
es, and it hurt when they touched me and I wanted to
look away.

"Your mother needs rest," dad said to all of us. And
only Janie, who wanted to show off the paperweight she
made at school, started complaining. As for me, I was
thankful. I waited until the door to my parents' room
shut, and I could hear my father's calm voice coaxing
my mother into her nightgown, before I went to my own

room. I hadn't made my bed for a month, and there were lumps of hair and dust moving in slow motion flush with the baseboards.

The wallpaper my mother put up a year ago sagged over the baby's crib in the corner. I stretched out on my single bed. My feet hung over the bottom. I remembered dad saying once that trying to hang on to what was is like thumbing your nose at God, and I thought if I don't cry now, I'll probably end up hurting myself; still for all the blinking and wiping, I could barely squeeze out a tear.

I kept seeing my mother, with her long hair flying free as moon rays, competing with herself to go higher on the swings in the park across the street, then kicking her slipper clear over the clubhouse fence and onto the covered swimming pool. She leaned way back on the swing, while the neighbours, too afraid to come out, stood at their windows, and my father, sweating in sub-zero temperatures, negotiated snowdrifts to take her a winter jacket and bring her home.

"You always kill the fun," she shouted. He got her off the swing and bundled her into the jacket, while she struggled to light a cigarette. "You're evil!" she yelled, breaking free from him and tearing toward the pool.

My father never moved quickly, but on this day I remember him racing as he lunged after her, bringing her down just as her fingers clasped the empty metal triangles of the fence.

Later, after the police left our house, I heard her quavering voice trying to make sense out of what had happened.

"It just feels like the whole world's losing its magic and I have to hang on."

"I know," I heard my father say, and imagined him holding her injured hand, and felt for a second like someone had punched me.

Sometimes I wanted to explode, to slap my father and ask him how he could possibly say he knew what she was talking about? I wanted to tell my mother to get out of the house and never come back. It scared me.

When my mother fell asleep, my father came into my room. He sat at the bottom of my bed, and tucked my feet into his lap. Even in darkness, I could see the two glistening streaks of tears running down the sides of his nose.

Once my mother dressed like a nun and told me she planned to elope with God. She knelt down on the kitchen floor, kissing rosary beads, praying for God to hurry and free her from screaming babies and children she didn't love.

It was the first time I ever saw my father cry. He followed me into my bedroom and wrapped his arms around me like cellophane until I thought I'd suffocate.

"You know she doesn't mean it, Annette" he told me, the taste of his tears invading my lips. "She doesn't even know what she's saying."

There was a lump in my throat all the time he stood there stroking my shoulders, crying, begging me to forgive her. The lump seemed to sit there like a bath stopper, holding everything in, and I wanted to push him away, but felt so sad I couldn't.

Now, my father's sobs were inaudible. His soft fingers pressed against my toes and the balls of my feet, and I looked toward the crib. A mobile hung from the ceiling. Colourful gingham fish, bright plastic beads, large blue and orange buttons. Derek's stiff arms reached, and I imagined the expression of continual surprise on his face.

"He is a beautiful baby. A beautiful child," everyone said, and I was so proud to take him out in the buggy, wheel him far away where no one knew who he was, only that he was beautiful.

Sometimes I would lift him out of his stroller, caress his back, tapping gently to soothe him. In the summer, I would bring a bottle and we would stroll for miles until he seemed hot, and then I'd find a shade tree and lay him on the cool ground.

It seemed like a dream. As if I had dreamed everything. And as my father's hands pushed circles into my shins, I wished I could wake up.

"Don't hate her, Annette," I thought I heard my father say before he left my room, but the words seemed to hover somewhere over me.

When I closed my eyes to sleep I saw her. In bobbysocks and a plaid skirt, talking and giggling about a boy she had loved in high school. In a gaberdine coat, playing hide-and-seek with my little sisters who didn't know who she was. In her smooth-faced serenity she could have been anyone but herself, and I could have loved her for that alone, but then I would see another face, a turbulent angry face, and know I could never love her.

It was early the next morning that she came into my room. "Your father is inhuman. He's an alien. Why do you think he does the things he does? Run away Annette. It's not too late." She was pulling clothes from the hangers in my closet and pushing them into a brown paper sack.

"He's taken my soul, but you can save yourself."

Derek woke up and started screaming from his crib, then my father appeared at the doorway with a bottle of pills, his face droopy and wounded, and my mother laughed frantically, "Speak of the devil."

I tried to make a cocoon from my bedsheets for Derek and me, a place we could hide away from her shrieking and my father's resignation.

Derek smelled of sour milk and honey. I curled around him, holding him with my body. Holding him so close that voices couldn't touch him.

"I know what you get up to with her!" my mother screeched, the hardness of her words cutting me. "Come take your medication," my father said evenly.

"Drugging me won't make me blind."

There was a sound of wood shattering, of crashing and banging. I held Derek so tightly it seemed we had the same flesh.

"Annette?" I heard my father say. His voice filled the entire room. "I love you, and I want you to be happy."

I tightened my arms around Derek's neck and held him even closer. I held him so near I could no longer feel his moist breath, so secure, I could forget to hear him cry.

ANNA,
I LOVE YOU

Gnarled leaves slap the windows, making sounds like green piano keys. My mother leans from the kitchen, points to her Lady Elgin watch, a smile hangs on her lips. She raises her thin arched pencilled brows, and so my fingers work the scales again, my ears listening to them ladder.

My heart is a metronome out of rhythm beating for Anna. Outside, the world is a wind tunnel. Branches from oaks crash and splinter just beyond our house, but I know she will come because she is afraid of nothing. Her dark hair fanning behind her like a mane, the snaps on her red vinyl jacket brushing against her electric arms. I see her, Anna, always in motion.

These notes are particularly happy today because I play them for Anna. My fingers dance like chorus girls. "Chorus girls for Jesus," as Anna would say, and I grin, tickling the white keys, thinking of her.

For lunch, my mother makes tiny watercress and ham sandwiches, bakes oatmeal cookies, and as a special treat fixes Anna's favourite, devilled eggs.

It doesn't matter that Anna hasn't been saved yet, or even that the entire congregation calls her "heathen"; my mother says, "Christian charity begins at home," and "Do unto others as you'd have done unto yourself."

My mother washes the good china cups in water that smells of lemon and bleach and is hot enough to take the skin off knuckles. The table is set with our best lace cloth. And I tremble thinking this is all just for us. Just for Anna and me.

When the doorbell chimes, I race to answer it. How could I have missed her striding up the path?

My mother says my name with a paralyzing staccato. "Ruth!" Her eyes restrain me. She is telling me to be more lady-like, calmer. She is telling me that I must set an example. She says all this without sound. Self-conscious, I slow my skipping feet, rein them in, open the door for Anna, my best friend Anna. Anna banana.

Her long black hair, strands clinging to her cheeks, is knotted under a floppy red hat. Her mouth stretches so broadly across her face her eyes nearly disappear. She flings her vinyl coat onto the floor; tiny, crumbling twigs shake themselves free from her clothing and litter the hallway. "Hang the coat in the vestibule, Ruth," my mother says. "Get the carpet sweeper while you're there."

Anna doesn't take her hat off before she comes into our dining room. My mother clears her throat, looks at Anna's head, and waits for something to happen.

"Aren't you forgetting something, dear?" she finally asks. But Anna says she has to keep it on, she's setting a world's record. She sits at the head of the table, her long, strong arm reaching for the plate of devilled eggs even before we've finished saying Grace. My mother clears her throat, then chokes, but even that doesn't stop Anna.

When all the eggs on the plate are gone, my mother asks if Anna might like to see my bedroom. It's a big room, with a large, lacy canopy bed, two white cane chairs with rosebud pillows on the seats, and a long clean dressing table, with a Bible and a wood carving of Noah's Ark on top. My mother decorated this room herself. "It is a proper little lady's room," she says. I close the door silently, tiptoe to the window, and pull the dainty eyelet curtains shut.

Although we're supposed to talk about ways the church youth group might raise funds for the Zambia mission, both Anna and I collapse on the bed, giggling. At Bible School the only chance we get to talk is when we hide together in the bathroom, but today we're here, just Anna and I, and I'm aching to tell her my secret.

Anna pretends to be our minister. She wrinkles her nose and sticks her teeth out. She shuts her eyes so they appear as two half moons. She takes me by the shoulders, pulling me close to her. Her hands move down my dress. "Ruth," she whispers. Her breath is sweet. "Do you want to be saved?" She looks into my eyes. Her eyes are the deepest brown I've ever seen.

"I want to show you something," I tell her.

"Bigger than a bread box?" she asks.

I roll off the bed, carefully slide one of the cane chairs into the closet and hoist myself up. I push the small square of painted wood away and wriggle through to the warm, dark attic.

"Be careful," I warn, "keep your body on the beams."

The only light sprinkles through four inches of mesh wire screen surrounding an aluminum vent. There is a silence up here, even during windstorms. It hangs heavy and quiet, and when you breathe it in, it makes you calm.

Anna and I lift our legs through the square hole and gently drop the board back in place. When we finally speak, our voices sound unfamiliar.

"This is the place I come to be alone," I whisper, reaching toward Anna. "It's also the place I keep my treasure."

Anna's skin is like smooth cool rock. Her hair, like unrippling water.

"I love you, Anna!" I say inside myself, and move to the corner of the attic where the roof descends.

Anna's shining eyes follow me, although I no longer see them. I touch a dark green garbage bag and plastic stretches under my fingers.

"What is it?" Anna's voice is a whisper ready to burst. I imagine her fidgeting, rocking gently on the wooden beams.

Dappled light rains like salt from the ceiling, staining our faces. "Is it a present from the minister?"

"No. I told you. This is treasure!" I say and untie the bag.

There's a crumpled note at the top, an old glove, some small triangles of pink construction paper.

"Did it hurt?" Anna asks, "When he did it to you?"

Branches tap the roof, but they sound muffled, quiet. I pull more out of the bag, hoping Anna will see: a white gym sock, a piece of chewed gum in a silver wrapper, a broken stick.

"Did you know what he was doing?"

I pull out a yellow pencil, bitten at the end, a dog-eared pocket Bible, and finally a red heart cut from Christmas paper that Anna gave me last year.

"But that's my heart," she says, at last seeing everything, knowing that everything belongs to her.

I want to tell her I hide it here, in my secret place, because I love her. That I think about her every day. I want to hug and kiss her, but my mother is shouting beneath us, and Anna has already lifted the board. Anna's face is as red as her hat, as she lowers herself from the attic and my eyes refuse to meet my mother's.

"What were you doing up there? Why did you pull the curtains shut, Ruth?"

My words evaporate; I look at the ground, at the bedroom light reflecting off my shoes. My mother's eyes narrow. Tears roll down Anna's cheeks. Outside, the wind rips up the world. My mother pushes me toward the piano.

CELLAR DUST

I'm in the cellar jumping rope. My shiny shoes are click-ety-clacking like patent leather bones, and even though I know it's wrong to swear, I'm damned happy. So god-damned happy down here with these damned old oak roots that look like dirty fingers, cracking open clay bricks, busting them apart like there was gold in the centre.

Hard to believe that someone spent days down here lining them up making sure they were straight, sticking them in place. And thinking, maybe, "This good old sturdy wall's gonna last forever."

Damn, I like to see them bricks ka-thunk, they remind me of teeth coming out, and sound like heads rolling around fresh off guillotine blades, but I'd never say so.

If you talk that way, someone always says, "they'll be sending a white wagon for you," and even though they're smiling, you know they start watching you extra close.

My feet crack down on cement. My clean white Sunday school shoes, the ones I'm supposed to walk extra careful in 'cause they leave big black streaks on tiles, dance like they're haunted, and even though I can't see it, I know hell fire's burning into my heels, chasing up my spine, like a damned mouse up a drain pipe, and I think of the musty smelling powder rising all around me like flakes of dead white skin, the kind you find sometimes in your Nana's bed sheets.

I think if you could get hold of this damn stuff fresh and see it in the daylight, it would really be a kind of mold green, and you'd have to bury it or it'd make you puke. But even if it did make me puke, I don't think I could promise I'd bury it. I think I'd want to hang on to it because, like Auntie Betty says, you never know when something's going to be useful.

Auntie Betty collects plastic margarine containers and aluminum pie plates. She scrubs and slices through the tops of empty plastic milk bags that smell like rotten cheese 'cause she says they're good for freezing, and some day she might run out of the store-bought freezer bags she keeps in the pantry.

If you open a cupboard to get a glass for water, you gotta hunt through a forest of empty ice cream buckets, glass jars, cookie tins. You can almost count on getting smacked in the head by some damn thing or another she's saving. And upstairs, in the attic, she's got even more stuff like this. Boxes and boxes of it.

Before dad left, he said this was because Auntie Betty lived through a depression, but my mom lived through lots of depressions. She used to go into the hospital once every four months and get her brains fried, is how she described it, but I never remember her collecting anything, unless you consider all the pills she took as a kind of collection.

She wasn't big on filling up space like Auntie Betty. Our house was a real skinny one, with hardly any furniture, and a rug that never seemed to go far enough over the floor, and cold walls. The only place where there was too much of anything was the bathroom medicine cabinet, and I remember how if you pulled yourself up on the vanity to make faces at yourself or pick your nose in the mirror, sometimes you might accidentally shake a couple of loose pills out into the wash basin, where you could watch the little drip from the tap dissolve them.

Anyway, if I was able to find a way to save this pukey green cellar dust, I think it would be a lot more useful than pills or plastic.

Auntie Betty told me the Bible says it's wrong to think, but if I had this damn stuff, I think I'd sneak it into the lunch bags of all those snotty-faced doughheads in my class who stand in a circle at recess instead of playing, talking about training bras and their mothers' hysterectomies.

Christine Cross is the absolute worst. "You can't expect Joy to know anything, she doesn't have a mother!" Like that's some damn big secret.

"Oh yeah, cross-eyes," I say to her. "Just 'cause I don't have a mother doesn't mean I don't know a lot of gross stuff." And then I tell them how Auntie Betty got four of her fingers lopped off at a canning factory, and even though it happened so long ago, she still can't stand the sight of canned asparagus, 'cause it always reminds her of green fingers. Then they all squeal and twist their faces up and cover their ears, like I said something awful, when I didn't even get to the part about how the whole damned factory had to hunt for fingers and finally found them two days later in a can of creamed corn.

I'd also put some of the puke-dust into my teacher's lunch bag. She's just like Christine Cross, except bigger. She never calls on me when I raise my hand, though there's no way she can miss me waving it around like I do. And then, when I'm looking out the window, she says, "Joy?" like she really expects me to answer her stupid question when she knows I didn't even hear the damn thing.

Whenever I hand in any work, she always hands it back with red question marks all over it, and keeps me in after school, 'cause she says I don't pay attention. But I do pay attention. Maybe not to all the boring stupid things she says, but I sure as hell pay attention to everything else.

I know Auntie Betty tells me I shouldn't see what other people don't, and if I do, I should forget about it, but I'll never forget seeing Mrs. Rainboth shoving a pair of really big bat wings under her jacket when she didn't think anyone was looking and fixing her damned hair piece just so over those two spiky horns. I've spied on her in the staff room. She takes off her tinted contact lenses, and her eyes are completely blood red, and if you forget your homework, she sends a beam of electricity through you that would make even lightning forget its name. And as long as I live, I'll never forget any of this, no matter what Auntie Betty tells me, no matter if it's in my imagination or not, and I do pay attention.

I'd also put a big heaping teaspoon of puke-dust into Ellen's cereal bowl. Ellen used to be my sister Nell, till she started high school and got her damn period. Now all she does is talk on the phone about boys. I barely ever get to say anything to her, and when I do, she's usually either all pie-eyed and swoony and can't hear a word I say, or if she does hear me, she just calls me sick in that pinched-in, prissy voice all the girls at her school have.

I told Auntie Betty I think Nell's gone to live with the space aliens, but Auntie Betty says the Bible says you shouldn't think, and it's wrong to be disrespectful. I don't see why bleeding from your private parts should suddenly make you a completely different person, but when I say this to Ellen, she says that's because I don't know anything about life.

She spends hours in the bathroom and doesn't even take a book with her. Auntie Betty says young women need their privacy, but sometimes I peek through the keyhole anyway and watch her standing naked in front of the mirror, puckering up her mouth and whispering, "I love you" to someone I can't see. It's so creepy it makes the damned bones in my back shiver, and I just know she's talking to an alien man, who's real tall and good looking, but when you take his human mask off, you see he's really just made of goopy wet phlegm.

You couldn't get me to fall for it, even if I was bleeding from my private parts. I know all about space aliens and the way they get you into their UFOs, and experiment on you and move into your body. Auntie Betty pretends she doesn't know anything about it, but I've read those newspapers she sneaks home from the grocery store and hides in her night table under the Bible. She knows all right, even if she isn't saying.

Whenever I tell Nell she better be careful, that the aliens are probably already in the process of cleaning out her body and getting ready to move in, she just says, "Don't be such a moron. And don't call me Nell."

When she was Nell, she never slammed doors in my face. Sometimes, after I had a nightmare, she even let me sleep in her bed with stuffed animals. Now she's Ellen, she's packed all her stuffed animals away, put them up in the attic with Auntie Betty's boxes of plastic and hung all these posters of boys all over her walls. I wouldn't even set foot in her room now at night. It's too scary.

But I think a few good doses of puke-dust might fix Nell. Aliens aren't idiots. Who'd want to live in a body that was always puking?

Auntie Betty says I ought to pray to God to forgive me for swearing and thinking, but I can't really seem to give a damn about God, even though I know I'm supposed to, just like I can't make myself feel punished down here in the cellar, skipping this rope that I'm not even supposed to have, looking at all these broken bricks, just waiting for the roots of that old oak tree outside to smash the next one open.

I think maybe if I could live through a depression, like Auntie Betty, maybe I'd feel different, but then I think of my mother and all her depressions and how everyone said at her funeral she'd never find a place with God 'cause she stuck her head in the gas oven she hated to cook in, and she had two small children to look after, and God would never forgive her 'cause, besides being a sin, it was also selfish, so I guess she really couldn't have given a damn about God either.

Sometimes I beg Auntie Betty not to make me go down into the cellar. I beg her to let me stay upstairs and have tea and biscuits with her and Nana and the minister. I even promise not to laugh if Nana farts or wets herself because I really do want to be punished because Auntie Betty says being punished is the only way to understanding God's love, and I sure as hell would like to understand that.

But she always sends me down into the cellar anyway, and as soon as I hear her draw the bolt across the door, and I reach the bottom of those stairs that smell like fungus and let my lungs fill with the musty spirit of mud that makes more spit form in my mouth than cherry sour balls do, and I see those broken bricks spread out in front of me like treasure, I feel so safe and so goddamned happy that I'm almost ashamed of myself.

HOME SICK

Dear Mother:

Today is the day we are allowed to write. They have let me have a nice pointy pencil. Mrs. Peelier is watching to make sure it doesn't accidentally slip off the page and into my wrist, like it did two months ago when I was writing to you.

Plaese oevr loko ayn seplling msiateks, fro sa yuo konw, I ma na iodoit adn cna nto sepll.

My handwriting is much improved since I have been taking the drug that makes my muscles relax. They tell me the only side effect it has is that it disturbs short-term memory. Mrs. Peelier is holding my head up so I can see what I've written as my neck is too relaxed for me to hold it up myself.

My handwriting is much improved since I have been taking the drug that makes my muscles relax. They tell me the only side effect it has is that it disturbs your short-term memory.

I hope you and father enjoyed your European holiday two years ago. I have made some friends here.

Mrs. Peelier is telling me that I ought to mention my new friend, Dr. Saber. Please excuse me for a moment while I talk to Mrs. Peelier. Mrs. Peelier just said that Dr. Saber has been my new friend for about three weeks and that he has been helping me and is very hopeful.

I do not remember this, so perhaps Mrs. Peelier will not mind so much if I write about other things. She is snapping that long tongue of hers against the roof of her mouth like a ~~rattle snake~~ concerned and conscientious care-giver but says she will allow me to write as I see fit because father and you know I am ~~a fruit basket~~ working to overcome my problems.

I am in bed much of the time here and used to think a lot about my present situation and become inexplicably depressed. Now, due to the drug, I can't remember if I think or not, but still become inexplicably depressed.

Anyway, I seem to remember a great deal about being a pre-verbal infant. Mrs. Peelier is telling me that this is highly unlikely because most people don't recall being pre-verbal. She says she wonders, too, where I learned a word like pre-verbal. She instructs me to tell you to take all this I am about to write with a grain of salt.

I remember once you asking, mother, before we knew how sick I was, and you sent me here—I think perhaps I was around three—why I seemed so afraid of everything.

"There's nothing to be afraid of," you'd say. "It's only your father having a bit of fun behind that mask," or "I was just pulling your leg when I told you I was from outer space."

I know I must have appeared pretty foolish never to have gotten the jokes, and I realize how upsetting this was for you and father, who so enjoyed jokes. I suppose if I had been more alert, I would have immediately recognized my lack of humour as the first symptom of my illness, and we could have secured a place for me at this institution prior to my fifth birthday. I'm sure it would have spared you much frustration and worry. I can only apologize for my lack of insight but under the circumstances hope you will absolve me.

I believe when the issue of my fearfulness came up, I mentioned to you a memory of being alone in my crib with the blue lamb decal on it. You had put me down for a nap, and I heard the vacuum cleaner downstairs.

You suggested perhaps I had seen a rat, and that is why I had been so frightened. There were rats in that house, you said, "big fat hairy ones that could nip a child's finger off in a trice," and you also mentioned the vacuum cleaner was on because I found the noise of the vacuum cleaner particularly soothing. "I put you in your crib and turned on the vacuum cleaner and never heard you cry once. But as soon as I turned it off, then I'd hear you cry, so I'd turn it back on again," you said.

I recall now the growl of the vacuum and my overwhelming anxiety. I have somehow been able to retrieve those early memories and know for certain I did not ever see a rat. To have been so anxious when everything possible had been done for my comfort is a depressing revelation and seems to suggest only one thing: I was ill even before I could speak.

But there are other memories too, which do not reassure me. I recall the terrible defiant tantrums I threw—cheap ploys for yet more attention—when the world just wasn't going my way. I recall how you barely used any force to settle me and tried to calm me by running the vacuum again. Again, I became terribly frightened, and again, for no reason whatsoever.

I once went to rub the ribbon from my pink blanket across my face, as had become my strange obsessive habit and found the ribbon gone. I was unable to figure out what had become of it and grew even more irrationally frightened. It never occurred to me that you wisely had removed it in order to help me break this compulsion of mine. Just as you incinerated my plastic bottles and dropped my baby doll into the garbage disposal.

When I think of all you and father tried to do to help and protect me, to assist me in growing strong and independent, I am terribly saddened that in the seven years I have lived, I have brought such shame upon you.

I am so very sad especially that my illness clouded my judgement toward the two of you and your motives, and I'm working very hard here with the help of friends to overcome this sick, demented, paranoid thinking.

I know now that father never really raped me, and that you never really tried drowning me in the bathtub when you found out he did. I know now that all those nights in the hospital emergency rooms with third-degree burns, knife wounds, and the like, were all my own imaginative doing and had nothing whatsoever to do with either of you. That my memories are all spoiled by this terrible illness from which I suffer.

It is the vanity of this illness that keeps insisting my feelings and memories are correct, that I am not in any way mad, that I am, in fact, quite the opposite, when all along I know this to be quite untrue. I know that you and father have always been right. That I am very sick, very much beyond hope. I have been told this realistic recognition is very positive and perhaps the first step in getting a better hold of this illness.

Mrs. Peelier says my head is getting very heavy, so she wants me to bring this letter to a close. She says next time I write, she will rig up some kind of rope contraption so she doesn't have the strain of holding my head.

I can think of nothing more to say, other than I am on a muscle relaxant to assist with my handwriting, and its only side effect is that it interferes with short-term memory.

I hope you had a wonderful time in Barbados last year. Please let me know. Adn pelase ecxuse teh seplling—yuo konw I ma oot sutipd ot sepll.

Lvoe,
Stacy

P.S. Dear Mr. And Mrs. Brite:

You don't know me, but I'm the Mrs. Peelier your daughter Stacy mentions a few times in her letter. It must be apparent to you from Stacy's disconcerted ramblings that she has not made significant progress here—claiming to recall being "pre-verbal" indeed! And not listening to a word I say about it! Using words, which she knows a seven-year-old has no right knowing, let alone using correctly! Sheer wilfulness is what it is.

I can understand your frustration in attempting to ground this child in reality. I myself have been working with her since she was moved down here with the more hopeless cases about two months ago now and have been trying fruitlessly to do the same.

But then again, I see so many children like Stacy—I have learned not to be too optimistic. Dr. Saber is also working with Stacy. Why she pretends she doesn't remember this, I have no idea. Unless it is just to upset me. She's always doing nasty little things like this to me, as I'm sure will come as no surprise to you who probably know all to well the vindictive and spiteful nature of her illness.

At any rate, Dr. Saber has proposed an interesting course of treatment for your daughter. He will explain it fully to you in due course. You understand already, I'm certain, that in cases like Stacy's, there is never really any cure, but the pain she will experience from the treatment will be barely remembered.

Upon successful completion of her program, she will be able to lead a normal life confined in the institution, and given, perhaps, some minimal responsibility in the laundry room. Of course, she will remain here for the rest of her life—but I believe you know this already.

I also want to add that in future letters Stacy might recount other delusions which might be less than flattering to Dr. Saber and myself. She may say, for example, that she is being beaten or that we are responsible for the injuries she inflicts upon herself. She may also suggest she is being prostituted or experimented upon. I'm sure I can trust you to take these accusations in the same light as we did when she first came here full of lies and slanders about you. Of course, she can't help it, poor dear. Mental illness turns its victims against the very people who wish to help them.

Yours,
Mrs. Peelier

This Touching

Steamy clouds smelling of rotting rubber, mildew and cat piss roll into the kitchen. Every room in this apartment, every corner, every aperture, has its own smell, and none of them are mine.

The dining room, as the landlord called it when I first signed the contract, smells of dirty socks and pasta. One of the walls is papered silver, and in the summer ants as big as katydids sprout from vents and cracks, making geometric designs.

He told me I could do what I wanted with the place. Paint it any colour, rip up the stinking carpets, anything. I think he thought because I was a woman I'd transform it. "The last guy who lived here liked to drop acid, but I guess you can tell that by the decor, eh?" he said.

His head is the shape of a perfect peanut. His hair is long, and dirty and blond. He has a moustache that looks bleached at the tips. His teeth are stained with nicotine. He talks in the slow deliberate style of someone who has smoked too much pot. He is tall and, like many tall people, walks with a perpetual hunch. When I first met him, I wondered if one night we would sleep together, but then I saw the woman he lived with and knew we would not.

The bedroom walls are obscene, closest in colour to a suburban swimming pool liner. There is no dresser, but a double bed. The mattress is stained like a map of the world.

Every morning for six months I'd wake to find new spots, the size of pinheads, the colour of rubies, blazing on my back. But even with a magnifying glass I could never find an insect on the sheets. No jelly-bodied louse, no bedbugs. Not even a frog-legged flea.

The living room is bare and brown and dank. Watermarks swell the walls. There is a scratchy plaid couch, dotted with the chocolate scars of fallen cigarettes, smelling of formaldehyde. My desk is situated under a grey window that has one small triangular crack in its corner.

Stacks of library books brush the ceiling, coloured index cards—blue, orange, yellow, pink—litter the floor like a shattered rainbow. These things, a few personal effects, less than half a dozen chipped dishes and one black sauce pan, this is my contribution here.

I know the landlord wonders how I can live this way. He has redone his apartment. Put in thick brown shag carpeting, a new sectional couch. I listen, each night, as he and the woman he lives with make love on their yelping four-poster. Sometimes, I fall off to sleep with their sticky noise and silence still exploding in my head. I think about the way his woman laughs, the way they both talk up there as if they can't be heard, as if darkness could erase them.

Other tenants live here: a couple in the basement as white as albinos, thin as if diseased, both with coral hair. Often they twine like sunning snakes on the front porch, even in winter, and snub me as I pass. And the German lady who sweeps gravelly dust into the air like thunder clouds with her good sturdy broom. She lives by herself in a small ginger annex, displaying contempt in the music she chooses.

Some mornings it is yodelling she funnels, thick as phlegm, through my walls on crackling records. I pull on scratchy clothing. I own just two pairs of blue jeans, four loose-fitting sweaters, all the same style and colour. I've stopped wearing underwear. Stopped wearing socks. My running shoes wait by the door, high-topped, hunch-backed, forlorn.

The open books on my desk, due back to the library three months ago, contain words that must be read one hundred thousand times. I make notes. Drop colourful index cards. In the margins I make lewd and ungenerous remarks. Others have had these books before me. Their spines do not crack. These books have known other hands, other fingers, other eyes, some gentle, most cruel.

Berserk red spirals roll frenetically across a series of chapters on boll weevils. Black, loopy, semi-illegible letters state the sexual preferences of slugs. In the morning, index cards will reach my ankles, by afternoon, my knees. I go to the kitchen faucet, wash clotted ink from my index finger, feel sordid.

I hear the landlord snuffle a dangerous laugh, the German lady mutter. Their voices hum through the cracks in the walls, extend like dusty open veins. Last summer ants spilled out of the cracks. They overran my kitchen, swarmed countertops, rummaged through garbage, manoeuvred circular oven coils. One day, I opened the refrigerator and found half a dozen ransacking crumbs of cheese. I put them under thin glass jars I had intended to throw out, adding one ant at a time, to see what would happen, whether they would fight or kiss or stroke each other as they do to restless aphids, hungry for their milk.

It is not love the way they wrestle and caress, the passion of their mouth-to-mouth exchanges, the tender embrace. This touching, they cannot live without.

They circle the circumference of the jar, black threads, creating multiple helices, marching in endless revolution. These jars, useless and fragile, easily become an insurmountable, inexplicable hell. In three hours time the marching slows. There are frantic communications, expressions of aggression, a dissipated kind of incredulity. At the end of three days the ants are all dead, their withered bodies crumpled, their heads folded to the ground as if in prayer.

Their small carcasses come apart in my fingers. Their thin waists break. Their elbowed antennae and limbs drop like worn-out eyelashes. I make notes. I wash my hands.

My stomach performs a serenata. I don't keep food anymore, nor do I buy toilet paper. I have not been outside for several weeks, perhaps a month.

The landlord's feet shuffle. His breath is warm and quiet as he hovers by my door. I remember I have seen a can of cream of mushroom soup somewhere, perhaps holding up a shelf.

The landlord secretes glue from his cunt-shaped mouth. He rubs his face discreetly on the backs of my walls, hoping to divine my movements. His breath fills the cracks.

I curl the tin lid of the soup can back, dump the clumpy mass into my pan, add a splash of water, swill it around like a whirlpool. There are grey stems, sliced white caps, discernible among other congealed hunks. Before it's warm, I eat it from the pan, wiping my mouth on my sleeve. When I finish, I wash my hands, deposit the coated aluminum cookware into the rusting sink. I do not buy dishwashing liquid.

Two coral caps and winter faces move under my window like the peaks of unnatural mountains. I have bolted all corroded bolts, drawn all shredded curtains, yet my senses expand through every distracting split and fissure.

The German lady is a spy as well. Her broom scratches snow off iron railings, her clipped voice calls "good morning," and her words melt to consonants.

I pull the lopsided vinyl kitchen chair a little closer to my desk and turn a mute page. I allow my head to bend, my shoulders to roll forward. The lines of the pink index card blur.

At night silverfish crawl from beneath books, from under loose and broken skirting boards; their bodies like small thin valentines, have a diamond's sparkle, their antennae and tails miniature ferns.

Two hundred million years ago, they scuttled over rocks, just as they scuttle the cold expanse of this crumbling floor, in straight lines, escaping predators, with their slick oceanic scales. They feed on starchy substances, the bindings of books, clothing, yet can live for months without food, and if they should come face to face, as they forage, for a moment they remain still, and then like gleaming arrows, hasten in opposite directions.

SOUND OF SUN

Her slender shadow fell like a bar across my bedroom door. I never slept, though she thought I did. The eyes in my head were sealed against darkness. My shoulders, elbows, knees, and hands sprouted powerful eyes of their own. Eyes that could see beyond starched bed-clothes, beyond her sickly raven form, dancing through the walls, even beyond this place she brought me to.

In daylight she washed my naked body. I watched as she lowered the cloth into the sink and retrieved it drenched and steaming. The soap she used stunk of lard. She scrubbed the night away, leaving my brown flesh tender. Her cloth probed my ears, pressing into my stinging eyes, ripping past my belly and between my legs, as she instructed me on cleanliness.

Her bucket of water, always scalding, spilled over my hair, scorching it to the roots, and then afterwards, with a fine-toothed comb, she would tear out unruly tangles, which I would later surreptitiously retrieve from her pail.

In my dreams, which came not in sleep but at moments when my memories were heaviest with the tropical beauty and warmth of my birthplace, I was told to collect her hair also—to select the most brittle copper threads, to tuck them away like secrets.

Her eyes then were shiny and sharp as picks, and although she knew nothing of my dreams or the way I had come to see, there was always a wariness in her.

For breakfast she fed me thin porridge, potent with her energy. She would not let me leave one spoonful for fear her power might be lost, but later, when she allowed me to go to the toilet alone, I would stick my finger down my throat and quietly bring it all back.

Outside the bathroom, her anxious feet shuffled, and her ear pressed tight against the wood of the door; still, she was not powerful enough to know. Her true nature had been revealed to me, a simple child.

She would lecture me for hours about the importance of remaining silent, of saying nothing if by chance I should ever meet a stranger. Her smile was as broad as a monkey's, her teeth as sharp, and my body stiffened and trembled fearing she might lean across the table at any moment and nip me.

One day, when the wind blew dust like smoke across her fields, and my weary arms were tired of shovelling and sweeping, two men approached her yard.

I knew right away they'd been sent by my ancestors, as both had faces of jackals, and I laughed to myself, knowing soon things would change.

She grabbed my arm, lifting me away, but not so far that I was deaf to their words.

The jackal men asked why she had not enrolled me in school, and she, indignant, replied, "The girl is deranged, her mind is damaged, she is only able to clean barns."

But there are tests, the jackal men told her, did she have the tests?

Her pink face flared like a baboon's behind, and her pale lips crawled backwards revealing her monkey teeth. "I saved this girl's life," she said, "I risked everything for her. I've raised her as my own child."

The jackal men were not fooled because they had been sent by my ancestors and knew her nature also. One scribbled on a card and told her that failure to report for testing might mean they would take me away from her forever.

She stood at the front door with the card pinched between two fingers. I saw this beyond the walls that shielded me from the jackal men's viewing. My heart leapt with gladness, for I felt all would soon come to an end, and I would be returned to my village and my ancestors who wept for me, but as the jackal men descended her path to the wire mesh gate, my blood ran icy because she turned and vowed in a whisper she would never let me go.

The following day she prepared a broth of pigs' bones and herbs I did not know the names of. As she stirred the liquid, she made musical sounds that rose in the air like deadly night clouds, searching for my ancestors.

Her sharp teeth scraped the bottom of her wooden spoon when she twisted it in her mouth. "Good," she pronounced, holding me with her pointed eyes. "It will make you strong."

She ladled the broth into a steel cup and told me to drink. Although I had always behaved as if I were ignorant of her evil, she had taken to looking deeply into my eyes and now saw my fear.

"It's not poison, child," she said, a grin slicing her face.

I took the liquid into my mouth and found I could hold great quantities without swallowing. I thanked my ancestors for not forsaking me and expelled the broth later where it steamed like green tarnish in the barn's hay.

I knew when the day of the test arrived because I could smell her pungent confidence, overpowering as ether. She dressed in her most modest and respectable black dress and put me in a prickly plaid jumper, cut down from one of her own. Her smile was more broad and frightening than ever I'd seen it, and her eyes creased as she warned me to say nothing.

We walked many miles down dusty corridors flanked by wheat before we came to a plain square building. I was taken to a room, empty but for a desk and two chairs, and told by a man, who did not resemble a jackal but whose height and long neck reminded me of a friendly giraffe, not to be nervous.

He showed me symbols on a page and asked me to read them. Because I did not know how, he said we would talk instead. At first, I could not understand the questions he asked, although the words were familiar, but then my ancestors moved into my body with great force delivering the answers. The man smiled and patted my head. I watched him move through the door, and then saw him, beyond the wall, telling her she must put me in school.

Her prim face collapsed like an ant hill. "It's impossible," she said. "Impossible."

I could feel my ancestors roll gleefully within, tumbling laughter out of me like water from a too full river. She had tried to destroy us, yet we were more powerful, they said, we have outsmarted her in every way.

But that evening, as I sat mending sheets and clothes in the dim firelight, I did not feel the victor. Her eyes moved over and through me with new and even more potent suspicion and I prayed to my ancestors for immediate rescue.

My ancestors chose to be silent this night, leaving me feeling abandoned, but when I imagined my village, I became calm again. I knew that soon I would be called.

I lay in my bed, tingling with vision, while she watched me in darkness believing I slept. There were stories she had told, about war and starvation, about her people's great acts of kindness, taking orphaned jungle babies like me back to her country. "Brown babies, like blackberries or pebbles," she said, "as many as you could pick off the beach," and then she would tell me how much I owed her and how grateful I should be.

My ancestors growled when she spoke this way, they twisted inside me and sent venom to my teeth. But tonight, my ancestors were quiet. Even when she changed into a serpent and crawled into my bed, twining around my body, they did not writhe. I was transported far, far away from her, back to my home, where I held council in its warm green fragrances and was filled with the sound of sun.

In the morning, I was taken to the square schoolhouse. Her harsh whisper, telling me to say nothing, hovered at the threshold. The classrooms were filled with children, but I could find none there who belonged to my people. They watched me with suspicion, just as she did, and I wondered how coming here would make a difference.

The woman who was to teach us appeared at the front of the classroom. She did not resemble the jackal, as I had hoped. Her voice was quick and demanding, her questions impatient. She barked out orders that I could not follow, her words like nets.

I waited for instruction from my ancestors. I prayed to them, begging for guidance, when finally her sharp, webbed words caught me, and my ancestors urgently arrived commanding me to speak.

I heard my voice tremble briefly under the weight of this task, but too late, for an icy shadow descended from above, harsh as the whisper delivered that morning, gagging me. The teacher stood waiting. Her spiritless eyes were suspended like small flames as I fought for words. In the end, there was nothing but silence and darkness, and the broad monkey grin of the woman I knew I must learn to call mother.

LIAR

You dream about going to school, feel that twist in your stomach, that sudden tightening sickness that tastes like paste and smells like cloakrooms, and you take the snack, the pint of whole milk, although you want coffee, although you hate milk, although you are not allowed to like coffee because you are told it will stunt your growth, it will make your hair dark, it will blacken your teeth.

You take the milk and sit in the front row. The teacher put you there, she said, so she could keep her eye on you, and whenever you sit in your seat, you see the teacher's sticky eyeballs cleaving to your sweater, your shirt.

She turns, addressing the class, showing the holes in her head, the empty pink sockets where she now stores contraband, chewing gum, super-balls, magnets and penknives. No one ever asks for them back. No one wants them once they've been inside of her.

"This child is a liar," she tells the class pointing to you. Everyone writes it in their notebooks, recites it from the board. "Liar...liar...liar," the class chants, and you quietly, self-consciously sob. You don't want anyone to call you crybaby, you don't want anyone to know the teacher can make you cry. She asks a math question you can't answer. The class wails with laughter while the teacher lunges toward you, her contraband sockets pulsating, and says, "I see...."

The class drones "liar...liar...liar," and you're wrenched from your seat, dragged to the closet, stuffed in a dark rotting hole. The teacher produces a solder gun from somewhere, maybe her eye socket, details escape you.

There is more than math you don't understand, more than angry winking eyes sliding from your sweater.

The gun is applied to your ankle and shrieks its way to your knee, a silver thread trails from the gun up your leg, past your thigh, past your midriff. With sobering recognition it comes to you: this thread is not just a thread, it's actually you and what you're becoming.

The children crowd the closet, nudging, shoving, encasing you in restless exhalations, erasing you. They ridicule you when you resist. "Spoilsport! Suck!"

Beyond this moment you hear knocking at the classroom door. You consider your wire torso. Can you be saved?

Your teacher flattens students in her efforts to conceal the operation taking place, and as coincidence would have it, the intruder at the door is none other than your enraged Auntie Betty, come to give you a dressing down because again you forgot your Spam and peanut butter sandwich.

"If that girl's head wasn't bolted to her shoulders, she'd forget that too," Auntie Betty says, and some of the uninjured students titter because they know Auntie Betty is ignorant, because they know you are being erased, because your long wire neck is joined to your straight wire shoulders, there are no bolts, and your head is the only thing left.

Under different circumstances, the appearance of Auntie Betty would upset you. This is why she came. But you promise yourself if she rescues you, you will not forget your sandwiches again, and with as much force as your wire body can muster, you inhale a throat full of air and release what you expect to be a soul-numbing scream.

Nothing but a quiet rattle emerges. You berate yourself for not having considered what the state of your soldered lungs and voice box must be. What use is a mouth in a wire body, you ask yourself. The absurdity of your question infuriates you, yet in spite of everything you scream again.

Beyond your claustrophobic confines, you hear the teacher tell Auntie Betty she hasn't seen you for a week.

Auntie Betty's high-heeled shoes scuff across the classroom floor. "That child was born bad!" she says, "and when I find her...." Auntie Betty's voice trails. She is leaving the classroom, leaving the building, leaving you, and the children are laughing, squealing. The teacher pins your wire body to a cork board. There is nothing left of you, nothing to hear with, nothing to see with, but still, you sense what's taking place.

The children encircle you, they twist you, they treat your wire body like a toy while the teacher uncurls your hands.

"Tens, boys and girls," she says, pointing to your cabled fingers, and you know her cavernous eye sockets throb.

She continues with math class as if nothing happened, as if your ordeal and destruction were part of the lesson, and you consider, while she talks how she lost her eyes, why no one complains, why you didn't complain when you had the chance.

You wonder now if it's too late. Who could you complain to anyway? But when class is finished, the teacher vanishes, the children flee, you unhitch yourself from the cork board, stretch a long tremulous limb to earth. Your legs are stiff but not sturdy, and you try to manoeuvre your way to the door, taking great slippery straight-legged strides.

Your body is unbalanced, a single swaying rod, flanked by unbending poles, and you can't help but consider, if you ever do find the door, how you will turn the handle.

Just then, you hear a voice, nudging you with urgency, knocking you off balance, knocking you to the floor. However, the floor does not catch you, you continue falling, through the floor, through the roof of your house until finally you hit something, your mattress, and bounce.

"Get up," Auntie Betty tells you, impatient. And you see that it's morning, your alarm clock has failed, you are made of flesh and bone, but you are not relieved.

You are aware of your rumbling stomach, your shaky knees. Last night, you were sent to bed without dinner. You'd said something you'd seen, something Auntie Betty said wasn't true. And now you can't remember.

There is a heaviness in your chest, a pain in your head. At breakfast, you find it impossible to eat. Auntie Betty sits close, watching every bite that defeats you. "Babies are starving in the world!" she bellows as encouragement, but today your throat clamps fast, your teeth fuse, your selfish lips will not give. It is something about the egg, its softness, its membranous yoke. Something about the way it slides on your plate, and you think of your dream, your teacher's eyes, and see her twitching sockets.

You recall a punch line, "the yolk's on you," but can't remember the joke, and Auntie Betty pries your lips and teeth open with the spoon tip, flattens your tongue; you vomit up the slippery-eyed egg before it even touches your tonsils.

There is a mess to clean before you leave for school and you are already late. Auntie Betty calls you disgusting, and you know you can never tell her about your teacher's roving eyes and pillaging sockets, nor about the night you spent in a closet being erased. You know if you tell her she will call you a liar, beat you with an extension cord, lock you in a closet. She will forget to feed you, to give you water, to set you free, and your voice will grow weak from screaming.

The slick red vinyl chair trembles beneath your sweating body, its black-footed legs do a nervous jig. Something strange is happening here, and you think of earthquakes, of angry gods, of vibrating soils that sift gems to their surface. Your chair spins, levitates into the air. You feel electricity burn through your limbs, see Auntie Betty's startled face, disbelieving. She could never have done this to you, never have caused you this pain, yet the wet toaster smoulders on melted linoleum, your chair convulses a back flip.

You hover somewhere between home and school, somewhere between closets and chairs, and your rattling voice rolls out of your mouth, a silver fuse, into a world of laughter. Classmates surround you, your teacher's slippery eyes fall from your throat.

It was the eyeballs... the eyeballs lodged in your throat that kept you from speaking, and even as the words explode from your mouth, you know you are not a liar. You know that every word you speak is true.

THE BLEEDING DOLL

Agnes feared the darkness. It had always been so. And now, her mother began revealing this shame to the assembled company.

"It doesn't matter what we do. It is all the same. Night after night, she ends up in the bed between us."

Agnes marvelled at her mother's control, her voice and breath as flowing as the mauve chemise she wore. "But she's a big girl now...why you can see that... Come, Agnes, come stand next to your mother. Let everyone see how tall you've grown."

It would be wrong to resist her. Her mother's polished fingers twisted curls in the air. "Come darling, stand beside me. Let everyone see."

It was a small gathering tonight, three of her father's business associates, their wives, an artist, and an awkward young psychologist. These were the few who had come. Others had been invited, but usually it was not until the weekend that the house swelled with people.

Agnes stood beside her mother but could not emulate her smile. Her mother's neck was a steady column of strength, her face a beautiful impenetrable shield. So often Agnes had watched as she shaped her perfect eyebrows and applied her make-up in the bathroom mirror.

"Tell me, Charles," she sighed to the psychologist, sliding a thin arm over her daughter's shoulder, "What do you make of a child who cannot spend the night alone?"

It was a comment designed to draw the psychologist out. He cleared his throat, and when his voice finally arrived, he did not address Agnes's mother as he should have, but Agnes herself. "Is it dreams that frighten you?" he asked. "Would you like to tell me?"

"So the dreams you believe to be at fault," Agnes's mother said.

One of the business associates' wives began recounting a nightmare in which she was pinned under a great grey rock, and another spoke of her childhood phobia of spiders.

"It was the most amazing thing," she laughed, "I could actually sniff them out. I could tell when I stood at a door if they were hiding in that room."

Agnes's mother gave a brilliant smile. Her teeth were all but luminous, and Agnes slipped away down the corridor to her bedroom.

She had dreamed the night before of a house with a secret passage concealed behind a bright canary wall. It was a house she had never visited, except in her dreams, and although exploring was forbidden, she began ascending the dark spiralling stairs that led to its hidden room. But the dream itself had not scared her. It was never the dreams. She thought about the awkward psychologist, his young kind face.

A peal of laughter from the living room broke an invisible film of silence, and from somewhere, music began. Agnes imagined her father, tucked away in his favourite corner, setting up chess pieces, and her mother, managing conversation. From her bed, she could see outside reflections that stained the glass light shade in the centre of her room, so unlike the pale flowered walls that surrounded her. And sometimes, when she focused her attention here, it was as if she felt her body fall away and her spirit rise up to the ceiling.

Night's grey smoke had begun to fill the sky; Agnes's porcelain baby doll, Lily, rocked in a petite chair under the window, snatches of shapeless light making rude expressions appear on her face. The doll was a very fine one—her face, hands and feet so detailed, her lacy white christening gown and bonnet so impeccably stitched.

Agnes rolled on her stomach. Every evening before the night came, she prayed to God. She imagined Him a large, dark man, bigger than ten buildings, and prayed for His protection.

But then the night would come, it would wash over the city like a salty sweat, and a voice she did not know would speak to her—a low musical voice, unlike her mother's. Her first memory of the voice was a memory of comfort, but as she grew older, she imagined her prayers echoing off into silence. The empty world spinning upside down, her heart jumping like a cricket.

In the mornings, she would not remember how she had come to be wedged between her sleeping parents. Her mother, always smelling of gardenia, her father of mint. Her bare cold legs brushing against them, making them turn away.

"You must stay in your own bed, Agnes," her father said firmly at breakfast.

"Yes," her mother added, "you are too big a girl now, Agnes.... You kick and twist so, and put bruises all over us."

Agnes watched her mother fill a pitcher with juice, her father lift a bleeding newspaper. The sun drenched the kitchen in pools of orange light. Sparrows tapped at a ball of swinging suet on a tree branch in the back garden. Agnes nodded. At school, her head and neck were like weights. She folded an arm across the varnished surface of her desk, cradled her chin in her hand, and tried not to shut her eyes.

The paper before her undulated like white rubber, the ink from her pen poured streamers of sapphire ribbon thick as rope, and the thrum of silence chewed away the monotonous voices that buzzed.

Then the voice would begin, and sometimes she would see lights flaring pinions over the heads of classmates and teachers, the schoolroom turn grey, exotic green tendrils creep from blackboards.

She sat beneath a broken oak in the schoolyard at recess, examining the long row of stained bricks that crowned the building. Demon crows hovered, and there seemed no higher place to go. But then the voice told her

to lift her eyes, and she climbed into the vacant sky and
felt her body quiver far from the masses of children who
would never befriend her. She ascended higher, past the
clouds, ignoring their songs and slicing ridicule, far, far
away and when finally the school bell signalled, Agnes
could not find her way back.

Giggling children witnessed the event from classroom
windows. Such a show of brilliant stupidity and defiance. "It is Agnes, smelly Agnes, pasted under the dead
oak tree like someone nailed her there." And the teachers, all flustered and uncertain.

She was led into school, escorted to the office, but for
how long remained in the heavens she couldn't be sure.
Her mother arrived, her pearly pink lips designing a
graceful arc.

"You must excuse my daughter, she is tired. I tell her
she needs more sleep, but children, what can you tell
children?" And to Agnes, "Always in a world of your
own."

She led her daughter to the car, set her in the passenger seat like a mannequin, and shut her door. "Oh,
Agnes, do you know how you shame me when you do
things like this?"

Her voice was not angry. Agnes had never once heard
her mother utter an angry word.

"You must try to be better."

At home, Agnes rolled herself in her bed's white sheet
and prayed to God to be better. Her porcelain doll snick-
ered and mocked her, and Agnes felt guilty, for she knew
she did not love the doll as she should. The flowered

walls threatened her. The glass shade above her bed turned black. Darkness spilled.

She closed her eyes, listening to her echoing heart gallop. The small golden lamp on her night table trembled, the drawers in her dresser shook open and shut.

He was bigger than ten buildings and shadowy brown, and He would protect her.

"Open your eyes!" the voice commanded. Agnes opened one eye, and saw the tall dark shadow sweep over her room.

Agnes watched the amorphous shape retreating; she pulled the white bedsheet over her head.

The following morning, she did not remember how she had come to be in her parents' bed. She did not remember walking through the dim corridor or touching the cold floor with her feet. But she had dreamed again of the house with the hidden room, a door behind the canary wall, and the steep spiralling black steps she ascended.

Agnes pushed her ear against the door to listen. "This is the witches' room," the voice whispered, and Agnes woke with such a start it was as if she'd accidentally fallen.

"What are we going to do with you, Agnes?" her mother chided.

"This cannot go on any longer," her father said.

They sat, the three of them, at the oval table, drinking juice from purple glasses, as the reassuring morning warmed the kitchen. Agnes said she would try harder to be better. And yet, she knew things had not changed.

She had once told her mother about the voice and how it spoke to her at night, and the strange things it said. Her mother smiled, her pink lips frosted like cherry ice.

"Such an imagination," she sighed, "but Agnes dear, I think it best you tell no one."

The voice got louder, and things began to happen. Now, she would hear the voice in the daytime as well as at night. It would tell her evil things and stop her from paying attention. It would make her do things that embarrassed her, make her see things she couldn't tell anyone she saw. And God, though taller than ten buildings and darker than the darkest shadows, would not protect her.

She pushed her hands against her ears and tried to stop the voice from shouting: "Nothing can protect you." She buried her head under her arms on her desk, clenched her teeth so tightly she could taste blood. The voice stopped suddenly. The room grew still, and silent. "Would you like to be excused, Agnes?" The teacher's words trembled in the air.

There were mumblings in the fluorescent office, whisperings and furtive glances. Agnes drew small stars on the palm of her hand with a finger. Her eyes counted shabby beige linoleum tiles.

And then her mother appeared, walking as smoothly as a spirit. No one could resist her. No one could ignore her. Agnes tried to hold her head like her mother's, she tried to summon fire from her belly and light her face with the same clear, bright warmth.

"Come, darling," her mother called, erasing the world. And she took Agnes home.

When she was young, she had lived in an imaginary world as well, she told Agnes. She had been shy and sullen, and Agnes's grandmother quite despaired that she would ever grow out of it. But soon she learned to put her childishness away, clear her mind of silly thoughts, and go about the real business of living.

Her cool white hand caressed Agnes's chin. "It is really much easier to grow up," she said.

Agnes wanted to ask her mother if God had helped. If He had come, taller than ten buildings and darker than a raven, but she knew her mother did not like to talk of these things.

She lay on her spinning bed, listening to Lily babble from her rocker. She knew it was wrong, but she didn't like Lily. She didn't like her twisted little face and the evil way she laughed and the things she said in the darkness. Her mother had been so pleased with the doll, so happy.

"This is a very rare baby doll, Agnes, isn't she lovely? Look at her face, the expression in her eyes. You must take very good care of her." And how honoured Agnes had felt that her mother had trusted her enough to put such a doll in her care. Now the doll had to be endured.

Agnes pushed her head under a cool white pillow. "Go away, Lily," she thought, "go away...." But Lily only continued to make faces and call Agnes names.

Agnes tried to think of her beautiful mother entertaining guests in the front room, dressed tonight in a splendid cerise dress that looked like a flame. Her make-up flawless, her teeth dazzling, and her voice and gestures cool as ice. She tried to see her father in his special corner, and the guests excitedly buzzing around her mother like grateful bees.

The pale flowers on the walls of her room began to come to life, stretching their vicious necks out across the bedspread, and the night began to infuse the room as if it were fragrance. Agnes prayed the voice would not find her. But already bad thoughts were seeping in. "What if the doll were accidentally dropped?" the voice said.

Agnes hated the voice. She prayed to God to protect her, but His cold dark impotent shadow had crept across her room and out the window.

The voice made Lily's small rocker jump and the doll began to scream. Her scream was loud and violent and shrill and Agnes thought of her beautiful mother, her beautiful glistening mother, and how she loved the baby doll, and in spite of the voice Agnes unwrapped herself from the tangled sheets of her bed and went to hold Lily.

There was a burgeoning silence from the front room. Magenta, violet, indigo silence.

Her mother stood at her bedroom door, flanked by worshippers. Agnes could not see her serene composure, her benevolent warmth. Her face was covered in a veil of light.

Blood filled the chasms of wood in the floorboard, it made poppies of the colourless wallflowers. Two large drops spilled down Lily's broken face. Lily was bleeding all over her christening gown. Bleeding in anger and defiance, oozing thick blood.

"It was the voice," Agnes tried to explain, but her words were muffled in gauze and the hospital corridor, where magic fingers soldered wounds closed forever. Spiky needles shut darkness out.

Agnes is opening the oak door of the hidden room at the top of the spiralling stairs. It is a shadowy brown room, smelling of violets and dust. A dress form stands in the east corner draped in billowy flaming material, a pearl-headed pin pierces its shoulder. In the centre of the room is an ordinary woman, on an ordinary chair, facing an open window.

JOHNNY PATTERN

At times I think I dreamed Johnny Pattern, running wild across the pea-green park, limbs loose as a newborn foal, playing pranks on all the girls.

He sticks his hand in Martha's desk, yanks out her clear plastic ruler. No one sees but me. I've been watching Johnny Pattern.

Miss Clement asks why I'm grinning. I look at the ink stains on my paper, feel an explosion of cherry blooming in my cheeks. "Come here, up front. Tell everyone the joke."

I want to tell her it was Johnny! Johnny Pattern! One of his tricks! But my throat is so tight even air won't pass. Miss Clement says she'll write a letter to my mother, asks if I've got the devil inside. I see Johnny, sitting in the front row, rolling sparks from his eyes. I could never cry for too long around him. No matter what Miss Clement says, I still have to smile.

At recess Johnny's a crazy bee tearing up the playing field. He hikes up a buckeye tree, as if he's got wings.

"You're not afraid to come up here, are you?" He hurls a spiky green grenade that hits the ground three inches from my feet and breaks. A perfect shining chestnut rolls out smoother than anything I've ever touched. I keep it in my coat pocket, roll it around the palm of my hand. After school, it is Johnny, walking behind me, trying to step on the heels of my canvas shoes. "Back off, Johnny," the other girls tell him, but I don't say a word. I just keep walking with my lips closed tight. And when we're halfway home, he races past in a zigzag, up Toboggan Hill. I pretend I don't care, but I think of him all night long.

No matter what I do, I think of Johnny Pattern. I see him on a striped summer hammock, brushing my shoulder, my hair. I close my eyes and wish. In the morning I wait to see him ripping over the hill. He flies so fast his feet barely scrape the ground.

"Want to go skinny-dipping?" His sentences are short lassoes, and I never know if he's fooling.

He sprints away, down the clay ravine walls, past planks of wide white fungus and glistening rocks. In all the world there's no place half as warm or beautiful.

He drops his clothing so easily. I watch from behind the trees. I know every nook of this body—know it completely, and I want to jump into the water beside him and touch every inch of his flesh. If I can't do this, I feel, then the world will end. The sun will burn out. The earth will explode.

He swims and the air smells of cedar. He crawls to a jagged rock. I watch him turn on his stomach, then on his back. Is he wishing I followed? Is he imagining me? I'd give my soul to know. And yet I don't follow Johnny into the water. I stand in the shadows of the sloping trees, hoping in his lazy sighs he will say my name out loud, hoping so much it seems impossible when he doesn't.

Years pass and it's still Johnny. Me and Johnny. Johnny and me. Him, skipping up the front porch steps two at a time, bringing me an orchid and a sharp pearl-headed pin. He punctures the strap of the dress I made myself, hours and hours of stitching and ripping and thinking of him. Thinking of Johnny Pattern.

We dance as if we are joined. Our bodies seamless, twirl. We lose the world, we spin. "Oh, Johnny, how I love you!" I've said it so many times. Said it day and night, minute by minute, all my life. "I love you Johnny Pattern! I love you! I love you!"

The floor slips away from our feet, all the dancers disappear. The moon is a private island, whole and perfect.

Up this old mountain in his father's black car toward the moon, Johnny and me.

"Tell me you love me too, Johnny."

Up this mountain, black and snaking, tell me you love me before we reach the top.

Johnny's hands are silver. They dazzle with their power to glide, to take.

"Tell me now, Johnny! Tell me this second!"

The buildings below sparkle, the steady stars gaze.

Johnny Pattern has fire-engine kisses. They ladder down my neck, my back, right down to my weak heels, but they never stop the flames. I lie in bed, my blood evaporating, everything inside on fire. Ashes and teeth and bits of charred bone piled up in a small heap, that's all that will be left.

I even smell my hair singeing, see the brittle cinders fall and think, "Johnny! What are you doing? Why don't you stop?"

My mother touches my forehead, says I'm burning up with fever, says all last night I screamed for Johnny. "Johnny Pattern," I screamed, "Johnny, you're killing me!"

"Why don't you find yourself a nice boy?" This is the question my mother asks, the question my aunts and uncles ask, the question all the neighbours ask, but I just smile and think of him. Think of Johnny Pattern. In the summer I put on a new dress, splash cologne on my wrists and ankles and stand at the corner of his street, waiting.

Sometimes, when he drives past alone, he pulls up close next to the curb and asks if I want a ride someplace. I never say no, even if I've got nowhere to go. We could drive all over the city for all I care. Drive to hell and back. Talk about nothing.

Every Friday we meet at a hotel. I know what the man at the desk is thinking when he presses the key in my hand. I know what everyone thinks. But they don't know anything about Johnny. I trace my name, my invisible name, all over Johnny Pattern. He smiles in his sleep. His lips a shade paler than a pink carnation, and I kiss them. I kiss his top lip, starting at the left corner,

all the way along, and then I kiss his bottom lip. I kiss
his cheeks, his forehead, his neck, with a mouth that
does not wake him, a mouth he cannot feel.

I watch him dress. He is surrounded by light. A circle
of cool light stains the carpet beyond him. Calm light is
zipped and buttoned into his skin. White fire smoulders
inside of me. I see Johnny's face, hold it in my hands,
but it breaks like chalk. The punishing moon spies
through my window. I am in my own room, my own
bed, and Johnny Pattern is nowhere here.

He promises we will marry in the spring. He gets
down on one knee, just as they do in the old movies, and
opens a black velvet box. This is what I imagine will
happen when I tell him how much I love him, when I
say I can't see myself living without him. I've imagined
this for years. Maybe ever since I first saw him. Maybe
before. My mother holds my head and curses Johnny.
She curses him because she can never know him,
because he is a mystery to her.

And now it is me, just me, and I wonder about Johnny
Pattern. I go down to the ravine, smell the cedar air and
think of him. I imagine peeling off my clothes, wading
into the river beside him. And sometimes now, when I
look into a mirror, I actually think I see him. I think I see
Johnny Pattern, and I think maybe he's coming back.
Maybe he's coming back, but by the time I kiss his silver
reflection, Johnny Pattern has already disappeared.

WATER HEATER HEAVEN

I pulled my landing net out of the water. "You caught something," Nelson said, tripping over his feet to look into my net. "Holy."

I dumped my catch, but it just lay there. Nelson got a stick and poked it. Clear liquid trickled out, then he flipped it high in the air, and it landed on its back. We both moved closer.

"What do you think?" he asked. "What kind of animal's got no paws?"

He plunged the stick back in—hard. Gave it a good twist, then nudged it with his toe. When he saw it was an old hat he kicked it back into the lake.

The only other things we caught were the hubcap from an old car, a paint can, and a rubber johnny. A metal gadget on top of an old water heater spied at us from the lake like a periscope, and a twisted rusty tentacle lay still at its side.

Nelson leaned his skinny body against the trunk of a tree and rubbed his eyes. For a second, I could have

sworn he was dad, but then he dropped his hands into
his pockets and shrugged.

"We need to sleep," he said, trying to convince himself we weren't starving. Things were always worse in
the morning, too, when our bodies were cold and stiff,
and we were tearing off the skin we didn't cover the
night before because it had been bitten up by blackflies
and mosquitoes.

He limped over to our backpack and started to unroll
the old pup tent we set up one summer in our yard with
a foam mattress, and a TV set. I liked to think about that
summer, when the air was so dark you could hardly
breathe. I'd lie there shivering, thinking all I had to do
was move my hand forward and turn on the TV. Just the
thought made the place seem a little brighter.

Nelson made a fire. Some of the wood was green, and
there was plenty of smoke, but he didn't care. He sat
right in front of it, reading and re-reading the last letter
dad sent.

Dad was some bigwig now. He owned his own construction company out west, drove a Mercedes-Benz,
and lived in a big house overlooking the ocean. It hadn't
been easy. We knew how tough it had been for him,
even without him writing and telling us. But he'd pulled
himself up by the bootstraps, started going to AA meetings, got his life together, had some luck, and ended up
on top of things.

"I'll bet he's got a built-in pool," Nelson said, "probably a maid."

I tried to imagine our father with money, but I just

kept seeing him, a poor guy with a stubbly beard. That was the difference between Nelson and me: he could imagine things he hadn't seen yet, and I couldn't.

Nelson kept talking about dad. How happy he'd be. How great our life was going to get, but I was smelling October on my uncle's farm, and in my mind picking the biggest Macintosh apples off his trees. It was hard work we were going to miss this year, and even though Nelson said we ought to be glad about it, I wasn't really.

I knew what Nelson said was right; Uncle Ross worked us like slaves and could care less what happened to us as long as the chores got done, but still I wanted to be on the farm in October, feeling my body work, so tired at night I could have curled up anyplace, but having a soft bed to sleep in, and three meals to look forward to in a day.

Nelson extended his legs so the long one almost touched the fire. He reached into the pocket of his jacket for rolling papers and the half dozen cigarette butts he'd been collecting. "Do you think he's got a girl-friend?" he asked as he carefully shook crumbly little pieces of twisted tobacco into a clean white skin.

Just seeing those curly little bits of brown on that folded fine paper, hearing the snap of that smoking green wood, and knowing Nelson was busy in his mind looking at things neither of us had ever seen before made me feel a little better.

"Bet she's got real big ones," he said, holding his skinny arms out in front of his chest, "bet she's blond."

I tried to imagine her as Nelson did. All made up and airy, but I just kept seeing mom, thin and plain in a tired print dress.

"Maybe that's why he hasn't written in a while," Nelson said grinning, "a girlfriend, eh?" The twisted spike of paper burned fast between his yellowed fingers. He pushed his head back till it rested on our pack and closed his eyes as he kissed the end of his cigarette. A long messy column of ash dropped on his chest. "Maybe a couple girlfriends."

I put my hand in my pocket and felt my old leather wallet. Inside was the fifty-dollar bill dad sent, along with an old family photo I'd been carrying around and looking at every night since we moved in with Uncle Ross. I missed mom and just wanted to see her face, at first, but later I started searching it for anything I might not have noticed, like the tiny gold crucifix she wore that I almost forgot about, and the way dad slung an arm around her shoulder.

Nelson and I were babies in that photo, but I still remember when it was taken, being dressed up and feeling mom's hands fussing with my hair and hearing dad complain about having to put on a suit jacket. The way mom used to go quiet after she and dad stopped fighting. The way her bottom lip used to shake, while dad sulked and swilled whiskey and later started throwing furniture around.

Sometimes I felt like burning that picture, but I never could, even when it made me see the accident; somehow, that old picture still made me feel safe.

I felt weak in the morning when we reached the highway. I sat down a couple of times because the world was spinning. Nelson said maybe we ought to buy food with the fifty, but we were really saving the money dad sent so we could each buy a clean shirt and a new pair of pants before we went looking for him.

We got picked up straight off by a guy going all the way to Calgary. He was a nice guy. Some kind of counsellor, I guessed, because he asked a lot of questions.

"I ran away myself when I was boy," he told us. "I went to Toronto because I wanted to see a big city." He smiled and offered to buy us lunch.

I felt spit filling the back of my throat I was so hungry. When we pulled in under the golden arches, and the guy gave us each ten dollars for anything we wanted, I thought I was dreaming. I got the best hamburger I'd ever had, but I couldn't finish it. And later, when we were driving again, I felt sick.

"You gonna be okay?" Nelson asked from the front. I could see my face in the rear view mirror and it looked like a wax mask.

I let my shoulders drop back against the seat. Clouds floated over wheat fields, too big to look real, as if some kindergarten kid had painted them, and I listened to Nelson's droning voice, almost buried by the car's engine, answering questions about Uncle Ross and the farm.

My eyes closed and I saw Uncle Ross's broad back bending in the barn to pick up a dead chicken, his set face, and the pink feathers sticking to his square hands.

I followed him into the house where he lifted his shot-gun off the mahogany rack. Runner had been part of the family since he was a pup, but Uncle Ross shot him right there in front of us without blinking. Nelson told the man that's why we left. The fact was, Uncle Ross shot Runner six months ago and Nelson only got the idea to go out west and find dad last week.

It was cool outside, but the sun beat through the win-dow, cutting a stripe of warmth across my cheek. I won-dered if Nelson was going to tell the man why his legs looked so funny, or how come we ended up on the farm in the first place, but Nelson was finished talking. Although I was drifting in and out of sleep, I could see him sitting in front of me, his head tilting toward the window, watching the wheat fields pass. And I knew, for all that calm, even though he wasn't talking, he'd started thinking about those things again.

For a long time, Nelson couldn't ride in a car without panicking. It drove Uncle Ross crazy. But now he was sitting there, relaxed as anything, finishing the story up in his head.

I was telling the story in my head too. But it was dif-ferent than Nelson's, because I remember seeing mom and Nelson after the accident, while Nelson just remembers everything going black until he woke up in the hospital. They never thought he'd walk again. He had to stay in the hospital for a long time. He didn't know mom was dead until Uncle Ross brought him home. But I remember mom's funeral. I remember dad stinking of whiskey, and Uncle Ross about as mad as I'd ever seen him. He lifted me up by an arm into the cab of his truck and we drove away. For a couple of years, we didn't know what happened to dad, but then he started writing. Nelson didn't want him to worry, so we never wrote about the work we had to do, or the fact Uncle Ross took us out of school.

We'd probably still be on the farm if Uncle Ross hadn't called dad a lying murdering bastard, and Nelson hadn't pulled his knife. Now we couldn't go back to the farm even if we'd wanted to.

The man cleared his throat, flicked on the radio, and after a couple of minutes started whistling. He whistled more with his teeth than with his lips. The smoothest and most carefree whistling I'd ever heard, lulling me off to sleep.

I don't know for sure what I was dreaming when I suddenly noticed we weren't driving anymore and the day was dissolving. I think it was something about being too close to the sun, and I must have really been sweating because my shirt was soaking wet.

Nelson leaned over the seat and pushed at my shoulder. "Gary thinks we oughta spend the night in a hotel."

It was like he was talking through fog, and I tried to fix my eyes on him but they kept wanting to shut. He and the man lifted me out of the car. Their hands were hammers in my armpits, and I wanted to yell, but my throat was raw.

I felt the smack of cold bed linen on my back. I was shivering like a rotary hoe, and Nelson started heaping wet cloths on my forehead and wrists.

"Gary says he's going to take us all the way to Vancouver. He's going to help us find dad."

His voice snagged and seemed a long way off. "Dad'll probably give him a huge reward. Maybe make him vice-president of his company." And then, just for a minute, I saw dad, all clean cut and dressed up in a slate blue business suit extending his hand to this man whose teeth sparkled like night stars on the farm.

I tried to hold that picture in my head, but it broke apart, turned into mom walking toward us, lips redder than poppies, laughing. Laughing like I'd never seen her laugh. Laughing, and telling us everything would be fine.

LUCKY BOY

Yoshio manoeuvred his kite, his heart thumping. The glassy cord and his arm were one, extending and arching in precise design across the steaming fields. In the sky, his competitor's kite climbed—a samurai warrior with red eyes and a face like a dragon—but Yoshio was confident he would soon bring it down. He had never before lost a battle.

He twisted his hand suddenly, watching his kite, sleek and light, skip over his opponent's. He had made his kite of fine bamboo and paper in the likeness of a sword-tailed grasshopper, and had included a ribbon at the top so the wind would make it sing, but now the song sank under heavy clouds, and the only audible sound was the sharp buzz of his string, sawing quick and deep into his opponent's.

In a moment, the defeated samurai fell, twirling from the heavens like a seed to the crisp ground. The grasshopper did a victory march as Yoshio rushed to claim the injured prize.

His opponent bowed, although shaken, while Yoshio fiddled with the broken kite's splintered frame and tested the bamboo to see what repairs would be necessary.

At home, Yoshio had many kites. Some he had made himself, but most he had won in battle, and so had become quite expert in their repair. This new acquisition could easily be mended, and he was pleased and proud to add one so fine to his collection.

He thought of his mother as he strode from the field, how she would clap her hands together when she saw his prize. She had always told him he was unbeatable because he had been born on a fortunate day. "My lucky son," she called him, and he felt this was true.

One day, he would honour her with great wealth, he promised. This would be her reward for bringing him into the world. She laughed and kissed him when he spoke, ran her fingers through his hair, caressed his neck.

He skipped up the mossy slope of a hill toward its crest, thinking of his mother's pleasure. Both kites sailed behind him, and in the distance he was aware of the glowing reflection of the village. He imagined himself a grand emperor, and his lungs filled so deeply his chest protruded like a rooster's.

His mother stood on their verandah in her lavender housedress, the smell of sweet iris and plum effusing the small garden before her. She called to him when she saw him just beyond the new maple, but her voice did not contain the joy he was accustomed to hearing, and his most recent victory already began to wither in his thoughts. He released his kites upon the border of large pebbles that surrounded the verandah and went to his mother.

She hoped to console him, but her hands quivered as she spoke, and, search as she would, she could find little comfort to give. In the last few months, she had grown sallow. Her flesh had turned coarse and hung from her bones, and today a doctor had come all the way from the city to see her. Yoshio had forgotten. He had rushed off to the competition, his thoughts in the clouds. His mother needed expensive medicine, she told him. Medicine she could not afford. There was nothing to be done. Her condition would deteriorate.

Yoshio wiped away tears, although he knew it was wrong to cry. He would gladly give his own health if his mother could regain hers. He pressed his face deeply into her lap, sobbing, and this he was sorry for as well.

If only he were a grown man. A man of business. A man of the world. He would bring his mother the most magical medicines. But here he was, sobbing in her lap, a small selfish boy.

His father had been a great man of business. His grandfather also had been such a man. If either were living, there would be no trouble, he was certain.

The following week was misery for Yoshio. All his simple joys had evaporated into hopeless introspection as he prayed and searched his mind day and night for some solution. One morning, as he ascended the rugged hills just beyond his village in search of a peaceful place to contemplate, the frantic voices of boys and men arrested him, drawing him into the excitement of their circle.

He saw a young boy, no older than himself, clutching several bills, while another jumped up and down cheering. A man at the centre of the gathering stood by a makeshift table making bets. Before him, two brown king spiders with bodies the size of ripe plums scuttled in a menacing waltz.

The circle of impassioned spectators tightened around the small wooden table. Yoshio could no longer see, but he followed the cries of the crowd until they ended abruptly. The winning spider was lifted from the table by its young owner, congratulated, and promised a larger cage. "One day, when you have earned me enough money," the boy told his spider, "I shall give you your freedom in the woods."

Yoshio could not release the boy from his gaze. He seemed somehow a special supernatural being, speaking to the spider as he did. And the money he collected and folded away just as if he knew all along he would have it. The spider was placed nimbly into its thatched cage and fastened in. The boy left the crowd and started off to his village.

Yoshio felt a tight knot in the pit of his stomach. He did not want to let the boy or the spider go. His mind had already begun to weave scenarios in which he, Yoshio, owned the champion fighter, and through his victories would be able to procure the medicine his mother needed. But how should he get such a spider of his own?

He found himself following the boy down the hill back toward the village. The wind had risen and the sky had turned black. Rain pelted his back and shoulders, sharp as nails, yet he proceeded to follow.

The boy glided over slippery rocks and scraggy young bushes, as if, thought Yoshio, he had wings on his feet. It seemed increasingly difficult to keep pace with him. Finally, close to the bottom of the hill, Yoshio shouted for the boy to stop.

At first, uncertain what to say, he approached the boy as if he were a curious animal. Then, a golden thought emerged and Yoshio knew what must be done. He offered the boy all his kites in exchange for the spider. The boy resisted at first, for there was no money in kites, and he had raised the spider a winner. But Yoshio persevered until, at last, he wore him down. "You will raise other kings," Yoshio told him, "as I will build other kites, but neither you nor I possess the talents of the other."

And so the boy gave the king to Yoshio, and Yoshio, true to his word, delivered his complete collection of kites to the boy. He was not sorry to do so, and it seemed to him, after the boy shed a few tears at the parting, he was happy to be the possessor of such a spectacular collection.

On the way home, Yoshio spoke to the king, telling him of the future he envisioned for them both. His promises were vague yet magnanimous, for he wanted to outdo the boy in all things, and he was desperate to establish the easy certainty of the spider's willing participation.

He examined the creature, turning it while its elegant legs groped for stability. Fine hairs brushed the palms of his hands like lashes, and in its obsidian eyes he imagined reflections of triumph.

The boy had given Yoshio explicit instructions on the care of the king, his diet, and the curious ritual of daily bathing, which was meant to assure a supernatural toughness of body in the spider, as well as a purity of spirit.

Yoshio's mother spent her days in a darkened room now, rising only to prepare her son's meals. She was distressed by the absence of his kites, and when she asked him what had become of them, he told her simply he had outgrown them, that kites would not bring him riches; yet he did not reveal the spider to her, for he knew she would not approve.

At night, he crooned happy songs of victory to the spider; during the day, he tended to the most minute details of the creature's existence as if he were its servant.

His butterfly net, which had long stood in obsolescence, was employed for the task of collecting the king's food. Each morning, just as the sun had risen, Yoshio would creep from his house and take the cool, mud path to a nearby pond. Here he would follow the beautiful scarlet dragonflies with his eyes, watching them hover and sparkle in the air like his most favoured kites, claiming them when they alighted on rushes.

The spider devoured the dragonflies greedily, growing even fatter and stronger, as the boy assured Yoshio he would, and by the end of the week the king again was ready for battle.

Yoshio discussed strategies with the king as his heavy body trudged across his keeper's glistening hands, responding, it seemed, with his small, intelligent, black marble eyes. "You are strong and I am lucky," Yoshio whispered, "together we are unbeatable!"

He allowed the spider to crawl into its cage, and began to ready himself for the journey up the hill, where boys and men would be preparing their spiders for battle. But, then, he suddenly thought he would need money to bet, and he had none.

He felt foolish and angry with himself for forgetting. What kind of man of business was he? But he recalled his father, and remembered how he had told him no obstacle need be insurmountable, and so Yoshio meditated until the answer finally arose.

His mother had a small money jar she kept high on a closet shelf. His mother had told him if she should die, he must use the money to travel to his cousin's in the city.

He had not liked thinking about the jar. In fact, he had swept the existence of it from his mind, but now he happily moved to the closet to obtain it. He'd soon double this money, and then triple the original sum. He had no fear. He took the bills and set off, hurrying along the hill's path, explaining to the spider everything he had thought and done.

The circle of boys and men had formed when Yoshio came upon them. The cheering had begun, and money was being laid on the rough splintering crate where the spiders would display their strengths.

Yoshio dropped his money on the table and exhibited the king to the crowd. A hush fell, for the creature's appearance had grown even more magnificent than it had been in its former battle. A thrilling current of excitement stirred among the gamblers, as Yoshio placed the king on the crate before them. At first, he feared that no one would challenge him, but then a boy stepped forward, a boy much younger than himself, who cradled his spider in the oversized sleeve of his jacket. Although not nearly as magnificent as Yoshio's king, the boy's spider appeared sturdy and the crowd shouted for the fight to commence.

The younger boy spoke to his spider in such a mesmerizing way that the creature seemed almost his puppet, swaying right and left at his command, while Yoshio's king stood transfixed.

"With your strength and my luck," Yoshio reminded his spider, "we must win!"

But the king did not respond. Perhaps he was unwell, for he continued to stand as if glued to the crate, and the younger boy's spider had already begun to lunge.

"There will be a fine new house for you," Yoshio promised the king, "a house like no spider has ever seen before. And each day, you shall have two or three fat dragonflies."

But the king had no interest in houses, nor did he care about food. Apathetic, he remained where he'd been placed, allowing the sticky threads his competitor fired to create an immovable shroud of silk.

Yoshio could not believe what was happening. He wanted to bring his fist down hard and heavy on the competitor, to stop this barbarism, but like the king he too seemed transfixed.

The competitor darted forward, delivering a bite both sharp and lethal, and Yoshio watched as the former king collapsed, and the victor appropriated his body.

The walk home that afternoon would be the first time Yoshio would feel such great loneliness. He would go to his mother that evening and discover she could no longer caress him, and would weep by her side, knowing the vast misfortunes of the world.

THE CHERRY TREE

Hoichi gazed into the garden, his tired eyes refreshed at the iris's sword-shaped leaves, their bobbing blue heads and flickering saffron tongues. For twenty-five years, he had passed the garden not allowing himself a glance. There was no pleasure in touching forbidden things with eyes alone, and his wife had extracted a pledge: in return for her permission to build the shrine in the garden's maple grove, he would not enter the garden again. He could not help but think of her both with admiration and loathing each time he had passed. It was one of those unforgettable bargains of their marriage in which she proved the superior in cunning and wit, for in this transaction she also insisted upon renaming the former Garden of Seven Pleasures with the more fitting Garden of One Temptation.

She had not always been as shrewd. Moulded for her future husband's pleasure, any swellings of aggression or unbecoming sharpness had been carved away. The arts of pouring tea, placing chrysanthemums in slender lacquered pots, arranging herself appropriately on silk cushions, comprised her education. She was delivered to Hoichi an empty vessel to fill, which he quickly did—with bitterness. Still, the result was not completely abhorrent. She became his most worthy and respected opponent, and he marvelled at her innate intelligence and her delicate cruelty.

He had wept quietly while attending her funeral that day, knowing he would visit the garden before nightfall and now, inside the garden's gates, he wept again, but this time with joy, for pleasure descended upon him like the sweet nectar of waxflowers. All time stood still here. It was as if she had been chosen for his bride just yesterday. His mother wanted only gorgeous grandchildren, and Yuki, then but nine, was the only girl on the list of eligibles with the grace of a willow tree and the aristocratic beauty that Hoichi's mother lacked.

The first interview was conducted at a propitious time, and although Hoichi's mother found her future daughter-in-law reserved beyond modesty, she believed she would blossom, becoming a devoted mother and a wife who would not bring shame to her husband.

Hoichi agreed to the marriage as one might an insignificant detail in a business contract. The girl was indeed lovely, a pleasing ornament, and certainly had the training to manage a large household. It would not be difficult to father the children she would bear. There was little to consider beyond this.

Seven years later, the wedding vows were pronounced, and gifts bestowed on the newlyweds by both families. Among these gifts, the lush and verdant garden, which, according to the geomancer's compass as well as Hoichi's family's experience, was of auspicious construction and on fertile ground. Hoichi had spent many blissful days of his solitary youth here, and had once absently dropped a cherry pit, only to discover the following spring it had transformed into a seedling.

"Heed nature's unrestraint," Hoichi's mother told his timid new wife.

But Yuki did not care for licentious nature, and much less the Garden of Seven Pleasures, which reeked of the fetid odour of the decomposing Ginkgo plum and made her eyes and nose stream with irritation.

At the end of eighteen months, Yuki shut herself in a room far removed from the daily activities of Hoichi's house and grew pale. Her body lost its womanly curves, and her gracious face dimmed. Doctors of great reputation attended her, but nothing availed until the arrival of the servant girl Oi-tei.

During those bleak months, prior to the servant's arrival, Hoichi found renewed pleasure in toiling in the paradise of his youth. The scarlet snow of fall gave way to the mausoleum of crystal winter, and then the spring, when the milky blossoms of the cherry tree exposed their fresh pink nipples and perfumed the air with their profound incense.

Here, in his garden, Hoichi could forget his new wife's misery and feel at peace. He began making great plans to excavate, just beyond the pine bower, a pond where he imagined lotus blossoms would grow and birds of many species would bathe.

In that first summer Hoichi began the physical labour of this undertaking. It had begun in his mind as a small spark, coinciding with his wife's unhappiness, and flared now into an obsession which could not be extinguished by his parents, in-laws, or the geomancer's disapproval.

"If only you would spend more time with your bride," his mother-in-law chided, "then she would have babies and be happy." Her words were echoed by his own parents, who blamed him for his wife's loneliness and suggested he hire a companion to share her grief.

Hoichi, annoyed by the outcry of blame, reminded them he had never begrudged his wife anything, and if she wanted a hired ear to moan her misfortunes to, he would gladly employ one. And so it was that his mother, who had heard of several poor families in the vicinity, began her search for the perfect young friend for her daughter-in-law. Again, she made a list, this time of eligible companions for Yuki.

Oi-tei walked with such natural elegance, it was as if she floated. Her face was so warm and light, she illuminated any room she entered, and her voice was immortally joyful. At first, Hoichi's mother feared she was an apparition and demanded to see her feet, as it was reputed spirits had none. Oi-tei courteously displayed them, dainty and well formed. Hoichi's mother, satisfied, made introductions and later that afternoon brought news of Oi-tei to her son as he laboured in the garden.

"She is like a radiant star, sent by the goddess, and your Yuki has begun to eat again."

But Hoichi was engrossed in his work. "If you believe she will assist, then I am happy," he said and sent her away.

When evening fell and the red of the summer sky began to erase the day, Hoichi relaxed in the still warm grass of the maple grove. He surveyed the serenity of the landscape. Before him, the cherry tree, a miraculous accident of his youth, was now heavy with crimson fruit, and cast glowing shadows upon patches of hydrangea.

It was then, while in the trance of that rare and complete beauty that the prayer to Kwannon, goddess of compassion, entered his mind. He desired a woman—not a frail hypochondriac—who would kindle and carry his love. And before his heart beat, walking along the stone path that encircled the cherry tree, Kwannon herself appeared.

Although his eyes ached, he would not rub them for fear she might vanish, but when he saw her lift her fine hand to the tree and pluck a fat cherry, he knew she was not a vision of the goddess, but the answer to his unspoken prayer, and he went to her without reserve.

Her lips were as crimson as the cherry she ate, her flesh as milky as its former blossom. He stood unspeaking for a moment, not knowing what to say, but finally it was she who spoke, apologizing for intruding upon his solitude, explaining she was new to the employ of the garden's owner and had come here also seeking solitude.

Her voice and appearance captivated him, but there was much more than simply this. In Oi-tei, Hoichi believed he had found his soul's twin, and from the very first could not imagine a life without her.

She had been reticent to become his lover. And he, too, initially felt torn by guilt. It was, in fact, this guilt that pushed him to be a more understanding and attentive husband to Yuki. His parents and in-laws marvelled at the changes: the growing maturity in Hoichi and the new radiance in his wife. They spoke of Oi-tei as a saviour, not knowing how she had performed such a miracle.

But it was Oi-tei whom Hoichi saw when making dutiful love to his wife. And every morning and afternoon, as he laboured on the construction of his pond, he looked forward to the paradise of evening with Oi-tei.

By the following spring, Hochi's pond was complete, and Yuki, soon to be a mother, radiant. "All my joy is due to Oi-tei," she said, merrily embracing her companion around her slender waist.

Hoichi watched Oi-tei, whom he loved all the more for having a genuine affection for his wife. It was as if Yuki were infected by her brightness. He had not imagined then that such an idyllic situation could be anything but eternal, and looked forward to the birth of his child almost as much as his meetings with Oi-tei under the blanket of newly opened cherry blossoms.

Oi-tei had always had an affinity to the tree. Once she confessed she believed it housed her spirit; and Hoichi then told her of its miraculous beginning and how now he would guard and protect this tree forever with his life.

As the date approached that Yuki would give birth, Oi-tei began looking frail. In all the time Hoichi had known her, not once had he seen a dark cloud cross her face, but now when they met in their timeless place, it was all she could do to keep from weeping in his arms. With difficulty she told him she too was pregnant and resolved to leave his house. Hoichi refused to hear. If fate were forcing a choice, his heart would not weaken.

He recalled the heaviness of irrevocable wrong, the vision of Oi-tei's head cast down, her nervous hands that shook the joyless chrysanthemums she held for her friend, and the sudden stiffening of her body when he explained to his wife why he and her companion must leave.

Yuki's face bled grey, her dark eyes fixed like a curse on Oi-tei as she wailed and bent double, breathless under the force of the first contractions. Oi-tei fled the house as Hoichi summoned servants, and then went himself for the doctor. After eighteen hours, Yuki delivered a stillborn son and laughed when they told her, for all the time she laboured she had wished it dead.

As Hoichi made his way through the garden now, he released the memory of his wife's suffering and instead recalled the most blissful months of his life. It was as if Oi-tei could be seen everywhere: beyond the pillars of the stone bridge, and then again across the expanse of lilies—just as she had been. His eyes lingered on the pond he had constructed in the mania of youth. It had been a poor plan. No sun ever warmed the water, nothing had ever grown there. And on that evening, when he left his wife and dead baby in search of his soul's twin, he had found Oi-tei, floating lifeless in that barren pond.

He looked to the shrine he had been permitted to build for Oi-tei in the maple grove. The statue of Kwonnon he had placed near the altar twenty-five years ago was all but lost in a tangle of weeds. Some of the russet leaves of fall clung to the statue also, and just beyond, where the pink hydrangea turned purple in the evening's shadow, the cherry tree no longer stood.

RUDOLFO'S CASTLE

Rudolfo's face was thin, his cheeks sedulous. When he sighed, his chest faltered. Juana had always been kind to him. She refilled his trembling mug with bitter black coffee, and did not object to the gnarling smoke that swirled from his twisted cigarettes.

He gazed out the plate-glass window of the café. Dry dirt crested in the air, and he found himself praying for the white of snow, for the islands of winter, which always at this time of year seemed so far-fetched, as if only in his fantasies they had ever existed.

The first time he had seen snow, he was already a man, his life, for better or worse, already behind him. And perhaps it was because the snow had been powerful enough to blind him, to bring a chill to his soul, that he chose to remain here.

He spoke of going to the Arctic, of building something for himself, a castle of ice. He'd laugh, once he said it, his voice collapsing into airless silence.

Juana made fresh, light tortillas for him especially;

she'd serve them while her hands were still damp from patting out *masa*. He did not eat much, he was an old man, but Juana insisted he eat what she made.

When she was small, not too many years ago, it seemed, Rudolfo had allowed her to climb on his shoulders. He galloped with her along the street, her hands clinging to his dark curls, her small body flying. There was no one on earth like him. No one who could bring such joy, and she felt now as she snatched the last sizzling tortillas off the griddle, it was her heart that needed to please him.

He sucked the steaming hot coffee and swallowed the tortillas absently. Juana wiped the counter with a vinegary cloth, feeling the distance grow between them.

He was not the same since his illness. It was as if during those months in hospital he had begun to disappear. "Where are you, old man?" she would ask him. "Where do you go when you leave me." She would try to bring him back with gentle rebukes.

It was his father he thought of now. His father's brown flesh, and the shack held together by a few rusting nails and cord where they had lived. He did not know why these images came to him. Why suddenly all he could see was the uneven dirt floor turning to mud, slipping away as the rain pelted through holes in the roof, infusing broken wooden crates, staining the large black seat of an old pick-up that served as a couch. There were insects as well. Armies of mosquitoes that attacked like spearmen with their fistular siphons, leaving wounds larger than stones.

And his mother, he thought of her too. She had been a beautiful woman. Too beautiful to have struggled so wickedly. Before they had been forced to move from the *vecindad* her spirit was alive and forceful. He liked to think of her there, but his memories did not always oblige him.

In the hospital, the doctors had encouraged him to speak of his past. He had even been given a tablet of paper and asked to write down any memories that came, but none were forthcoming then. That was in the winter, when the snow on the ground was like thick wool, and he sat in a chair by the barred window watching his warm breath meet the filtering glass in fog. How many hours he sat like that he could not say, but he recalled now the divine feeling of lightness, even before the first treatments. And then the thaw set in and the treatments ended, and he was sent back home to the trailer where he lived.

At first, Juana came to the trailer every day with food. She sat at the foot of his bed, filling the air around him with words. Words like small worms at the end of fishhooks, he thought, designed to catch something inside him and pull it out. He knew she would still be coming to his trailer if he didn't force himself to the café. And so he came, guzzling coffee most of the morning, eating whatever foods she fancied to cook for him, and smoking his own clumsily rolled cigarettes made from tobacco he hadn't yet noticed was stale, tobacco he had purchased before his breakdown.

Juana cooked fried eggs, sausage and bacon for the

truckers who swept into the café. They were large white men who demanded service and whistled and patted her in a way she had grown accustomed to.

Her father had been one of them. He had met her mother, Candelaria, in El Paso, Texas, in a restaurant not unlike the café. The owner had a string of greasy spoons and could pay illegal immigrants in food. When Juana's father first smiled at her, Candelaria took one look at his fine handsome face, and decided he would not leave Texas without her.

Rudolfo thought of Candelaria often, the way her straight black hair would cut between her curving shoulders, and how, in spite of the fires of hell, she could still smile her beautiful smile. Seeing her daughter serving coffee, frying eggs, it was difficult for Rudolfo to convince himself this was not Candelaria. And this, perhaps more than anything, made him uncomfortable around Juana and wish she would not persist in attending him.

Last night he had dreamed of Candelaria, that she had come in the darkness to his trailer, weeping. At first he had thought it wasn't a dream... that the woman before him was Juana, and he took her into his small bed like a father, holding her cold body tightly against his own, but he could not seem to warm her. Then he realized it was Candelaria, her naked shoulders glacial, her lips frozen, and he remembered, at last, Candelaria was dead.

For a long time after he woke, he lay restless in the arms of mother night. He saw himself a boy again, and his compadres, sliding down the steep embankment, wading together in the turbulent eddying waters of the muddy swell.

Now, as he finished the dregs of his coffee, he could see the great river again, and again his father's care-worn face, his mother's anxious eyes, brothers and sisters so many he could not recall their names, and he longed for the shiver of winter to fill his hollow bones and clean away with its subsuming whiteness all that was dark and poor within him.

His father had crossed the river many times, sneaking furtively in the evening up cratered northern embankments, sometimes sleeping entire nights in their holes so he would not be discovered by police.

He worked on building sites, in factories, on farms, employed by people who did not mind taking risks with the law in order to save themselves money, and then, sometimes six months later, he would return, always bearing gifts. For Rudolfo's mother he would bring sheer stockings and the most fashionable clothing; for the little ones, he brought sweets. Rudolfo's older sisters got beautiful hair ribbons, and for Rudolfo, the eldest son, there was always something extra special.

How was it now that Rudolfo still could feel the weight of these magical gifts and recall in such precise detail the most exquisite? The small black box, the transistor radio that spoke and sang, bringing all that was desired, like voices of angels, to Rudolfo's ears.

In *el norte*, people lived differently. There was money and food, nice things, and jobs. Everyone had a chance in *el norte*, rich or poor. This is what Rudolfo learned from his talking box. And this is why, at an early age, he decided he too would swim the tempestuous river and perhaps in *el norte* find his gold.

His father would joke about the prospects: "Yes..." he would say, "when I started this game, the police just called me a dirty wetback...but my son...my son...he will be much better than me.... Right from the start they will call him 'an illegal immigrant'!" He would stamp his foot and laugh, wink at Rudolfo.

And then the day arrived when his father was shot while crossing the river. The bullet did not kill him but lodged in his skull like the point of a dull knife that could not quite pierce an apple to its core. Perhaps it had been a group of redneck vigilantes, or a frustrated sheriff who had fired, no one would ever know the truth. His father somehow had been able to crawl back to land. The only people who could have removed the bullet were in *el norte*, yet his father was too poor to be helped.

The neighbours all said what a miracle it was he had survived. For many months, he lay propped in a bed in the kitchen, a gauze turban twisted around his head.

Rudolfo's mother lit votive candles and began attending mass again. For a long time, she had not gone because she said she was too busy. Now, she believed it was her neglect that had caused this tragedy.

Then the landlord arrived demanding rent money, which she could not pay. For a time they lived like rodents, hiding and delusive, but before long they were discovered and evicted. That is when Rudolfo and his mother built the shack. His father had to be carried there. Neither of them considered the possibility he might not recover. Both had faith he would live to cross the river again. And yet, every day his mind grew weaker until he could recognize nothing.

The heat of the day lodged itself under Rudolfo's skin and burned him from inside out. He could no longer tolerate the sticky prickly feeling of cotton against his flesh, and pulled at his collar, cursing it.

Juana smiled at him. It was a sweet, Candelaria smile, he thought. She brought him ice water and assured him that winter would come. She was Candelaria's daughter, yet she knew the words he needed to hear.

He thought of winter, of snowflakes like large white moths, encircling lanterns. He thought of the still cold earth. When he had first seen snow, he remembered that spontaneous feeling of joy. Juana poured him another cup of coffee, then turned to the spitting griddle. The smoky scent of bacon reminded him of winter too, and he rested his elbows gently on the counter.

It was almost as if he could feel Candelaria's luxuriant hair brush his face and hear her quiet voice. He closed his eyes and imagined her, but not as she was before death. Death's unfeeling mask distorted as it struggled to reclaim what life had given. To Rudolfo, Candelaria would always be just as she was, the pretty, young girl who organized dances in the *vecindad*. He would always see her at that age. Too young still to dance with boys, yet always so eager for their attentions.

He remembered the great lengths she would go to in order to secure a record player for the evening. Sometimes, it seemed an impossible task, yet Candelaria's determination would always win out.

When he first danced with her, it was behind the building far from her mother's disapproving eyes. Already, he and his family had suffered the death of his father and no longer lived in the way those in the *vecindad* considered respectable. If her mother had discovered it was Rudolfo Candelaria was seeing, she would surely have beaten her. As it was, Candelaria was routinely punished for being disobedient and wilful.

Rudolfo lifted his unsteady hand in the air, swatted at an imagined insect. The sweltering café began to shrink around him. He did not want to think of Candelaria's beautiful turquoise bruises, her glistening cherry blood. Yet these were the images that persisted, overflowing like exuberant tides.

Juana handed him a serviette. Her face was grave, full of concern. He had not realized up to that moment that he was sobbing again. He felt her touch his wrist. Her hand soft and cool as powder; he wanted to lift it to his lips, kiss it with a passion that would melt his flagging soul.

Raucous men filled the café with laughter and complaints, with smells and attitudes. "Stop making out with that crazy old man and bring the bill," some trucker shouted from the front. Juana lifted her head, smiled her Candelaria smile, patted Rudolfo's shoulder. The trace of her hand lingered. It made everything seem all

right, everything seem good-humoured. Yes, Rudolfo
could smile. He could smile like an idiot. He could smile
until his gums ached because he was a good-humoured
man. He had worked many jobs, met many men, and
always was well-liked. Even Candelaria's husband had
liked Rudolfo. "You're okay," he snorted, when
Rudolfo laughed at his jokes, when he offered him cigarettes, paid for his newspapers. "You're just one hel-
luva guy."

And how Rudolfo and Candelaria laughed at him
behind his back. How they mimicked him, "One hellu-
va guy." And he such a fool, believing all the while
Rudolfo was her brother.

Rudolfo lit another cigarette. For a second, it flared
and smelled of burning leaves. He recalled first coming
to Alberta in the fall when the clouds were so low over
the fields it seemed if only he could just reach high
enough, he'd capture one. And then, a few weeks later,
meeting up with Candelaria again, white crystals glistening like jewels in her hair, teaching him how to make
angels in the snow.

Even after all those years, her face and body were the
same. Her smile, her expressions, even the way she wore
her hair, all unchanged. But something inside had
become different. Something inside had become like
polished slate, and Rudolfo felt safe and shielded whenever he was with her.

She had never stopped writing to him. He had saved
all her letters and spent much of his time now sifting
through them. When she had first left home, she did not

have this core. She left, like everyone else, to escape. She paid a man to carry her across the river on his shoulders. She took the first job she could find. It was only after she had settled in Alberta with her new husband, Gordy, after several years of rough life, that this metamorphosis took place.

But it was not a coward's resignation to fate, nor was it a cynic's bitterness. If it had been either of these, Rudolfo knew he would only have been able to feel grief for her. There was something else. Something he was searching for in himself, and he combed through her letters, night after night, trying to find out what it was. He looked at Candelaria's daughter and watched it manifest in her. This core of something hard and precious, this was her mother's gift. To be like a nail and submit to the hammer. He could not be a nail, he could hold nothing together, and because of this he suffered. And yet, in the hospital, he had felt no pain.

Days went by, weeks, months, and he remained like an insect suspended between larva and imago, watching the world from a transparent chrysalis. Juana had come. He recalled her visits vaguely. The crisp cinnamon smell of her person, the strength of her voice. But all these things had been subdued, all existed now only under a pale veneer. It made him think of wooden fences sloppily white-washed, of the blinding blue hospital lights, of all the chalky grey cities he had ever passed through, and as much as he would have liked to possess the vision to see beyond this, at times it seemed the greatest blessing he could not.

He drew pictures in the hospital that he had no recollection of drawing. Pictures of soaring towers ascending beyond the outer limits of sky; austere angular castles with elaborate parapets and turrets. A doctor on staff offered money for one of Rudolfo's pictures, but he wouldn't let him pay. He gave it to the doctor as a gift. The rest of the pictures came home with Rudolfo. A nurse solicitously packed them, and Juana offered to hang them, but Rudolfo asked that she take them away. They seemed foreign to him, meaningless, even frightening. Yet now, he joked of building such a castle for himself. The men in the café laughed at him. "King shit," they called him under their breath. Some had known him before his breakdown; they drank and played cards with him, but never fully trusted him, and now were glad they hadn't. He was such a crazy bastard, always laughing and crying, waving his arms around, talking about crazy things, and they kept their distance.

This man beside him reminded him of Gordy. The brown hairs rolling on his arms like crumbled tobacco, the anxious knuckles of his nicotine-stained hands always eager to fight.

It had been such an excruciatingly hot day, and Gordy, trying to wash himself free of the heat, had been drinking gallons of beer. Candelaria was in the tiny kitchen of the trailer making dinner. Since Rudolfo's arrival, she took more care over the preparation of food. Gordy stormed into the trailer and grabbed Candelaria by the hair, smashed her head against the cupboards. Rudolfo moved to intervene, but Candelaria stopped him. "Get out of here, you ass!" she'd shouted, as if he were the one beating her. He stumbled down the trailer stairs in a daze, his knees vibrating as he listened to the splintering violence. There had been few times in his life when he had felt so helpless and cowardly, few times he had felt so rejected and afraid.

The sky that evening, he recalled, was bright with stars. He looked up into the heavens because there seemed nowhere else to look. He dragged his uncooperative feet along a path, out past some scraggy bush, lit a cigarette and inhaled as deeply as he possibly could. A lover's night, he thought, and felt a gnawing ache of desire for all he couldn't have.

Later, he crept back into the trailer. Gordy had passed out on the living room couch, Candelaria was collecting large fragments of broken china and glass in her stained apron. He'd asked her then to leave with him. He said he'd take her anywhere in the world she wanted to go. Her bruised face was bent low toward the ground, just as if she were praying, and Rudolfo heard her say "dreamer."

How much he had wanted to convince her of this dream. He still believed it could have been possible. But Candelaria did not trust dreams. Still, he persisted in begging her, whenever he saw her, whenever they made love.

"And what would we do for money?" she asked, "How would Juana be fed? Where would we live?" She would abandon Rudolfo suddenly in his dishevelled bed. At times, her withdrawal from him was so abrupt it left him breathless.

"We'd survive," he'd shout. His voice ringing with pain, even to his own ears.

"I'm surviving now," she told him.

After that first night, he began hating Candelaria's husband. Just to look at him filled Rudolfo with poison, but he was careful never to show what he felt. Sometimes, he'd wait for Gordy to get so drunk he'd forget himself. Then it was easy to pound his face into the ground. In the morning, he would lie, call Gordy "friend," tell him that three large men had set upon him from behind. But as the signs of Candelaria's abuse became more extreme, this kind of revenge became less satisfying. In the end, however, it was Candelaria who said she wished him dead.

Rudolfo's stomach was tight with grief. He wanted to leave the café, leave the world, wander someplace where these thoughts wouldn't follow, but Juana kept him here, and he knew wherever he went, she would hold him.

The man who looked like Gordy leaned toward Rudolfo. "Tell me," he asked, still watching Juana, "How crazy does a man have to be to get a date with your girlfriend?"

Rudolfo could not respond. He could not smile. Nor could he fight. His mind created sharp icicles to cut away this stranger, to make his words unintelligible.

"Can't he hear me?" the man asked Juana. He pushed Rudolfo. "Can't you hear me, you crazy fuck? Why the hell aren't you in an institution?"

But it was as if Rudolfo had completely vanished, and the man beside him, getting no response, became afraid.

"Oh, fuck you!" he finally said, giving up, moving quickly from the counter as if he might catch this madness.

Rudolfo pulled at the cloth of his damp shirt. Outside, dust formed powdered clouds and swept through the town, past the highway, over the fields to someplace distant. "How many months until winter?" he asked Juana, and she leaned across the counter, kissed his sweating forehead with her Candelaria lips, igniting the sky with winter pink.

"We could go away," he said to her, grabbing her dry cool hand. "We could go north." His muddy eyes were like two eclipsing suns and he barely felt the gentle tug as she slipped free; for he was already there, in the blustery circle of white.

THE CONFERMENT

The sun left the sky, and crazy blackbird clouds flew out of the dust. They hovered just south of the subdivision, and it seemed for a time we would have to abandon our homes, but then the clouds changed course, and the newscasters announced there was no longer any danger.

My mother and the housekeeper ambled about all morning and afternoon packing, then unpacking, valuables. I remained in my room a prisoner watching the street and its parading debris from my window. I recall somersaulting leaves and flowers, lids of garbage cans twirling like dancers' skirts, and feelings of envy and exhilaration as twigs and bullets of hail lashed our house.

While roof shingles rattled and patio furniture tumbled drunkenly over hedges, Riparian was forming in my mind. She had existed before my birth, before the birth of my parents, whose grandparents so many years before even this had excluded her, and I recalled the first time I heard her name, how it spilled into the tiny nursery where I played, floating like the smell of sour milk

throughout the house. I carried it in my bones, felt it
stretch and lengthen and turn thick and grow. It stayed
with me until the day she drove up our street in a yellow taxi, arrived at our door. "A spot of trouble in
Bermuda," she told my mother. "Things have suddenly
become awkwardish."

Mother paid the driver. The housekeeper dragged
Riparian's overstuffed suitcase into the guest room.
Father was summoned from his office.

My mother's snarl was hushed. Yet Riparian, or
Auntie Rip as she made me call her when no one was
around and she'd taken down the old British elocution
and dropped her skin a stitch, knew she was not a welcome guest.

"They think I'm filthy rich," she'd snort and cackle,
"but only half that equation's true." She'd sprawl on her
bed, dark and naked, one broad muddy foot hitched
over a knee.

My parents buzzed like summer insects all over the
house that year. In closets and other unlikely places,
their suppressed voices dancing and duelling: "When is
she going to leave? What are we going to do with her?"
My mother was always the sharpest. My father never
had answers. But Auntie Rip was rooted and wasn't
about to leave. She slept until noon, took luncheon in
the courtyard, drank Velvet Hammers compulsively in
daylight and smoked like a forest ablaze. Evenings, after
three helpings of dinner, she slid gaily up the front stairs
to her room, removed her prim white gloves at the
threshold and gave an obligatory affect-laden yawn.

When I heard her door shut I'd sneak across the hall, follow traces of her wild violet cologne. She'd be unpinning her hair, patting her face. "This weather sure makes things stick," she'd complain. "Come give your old Auntie Rip a hand, honey." And I'd help pry her face loose, so she could hang it on the peg behind the door, and unbuckle the skin at the top of her head so it would fall all in one, a wrinkled sack around her ankles.

"It sure feels good to breathe," she'd sing, and her voice was so rich I could feel it echo in my stomach. She reminded me of the midnight sky, her darkness swirled and shifted nebulously, and I followed her movements with my eyes until she told me to quit gawking, and she folded me lovingly into herself, a warm graceful river.

By day, we kept our distance, avoiding any show of contact, yet I couldn't help watching Riparian in her flowered dresses and full-brimmed hats. I couldn't stop myself from searching for the darkness peeking from her ancient face.

She was a story to be entered, and within her, I lived unimaginable lives, moments infinitely bound to all time. She laughed at my wonder, my serious surprise, "Don't they teach you anything at school?" she said, tickling me with ripples, pouring fountains of pictures through my mind.

But sometimes she would stop her playful motions and murmur sad observations about the world. Tidal waves of grief would swell over her rich, impenetrable blackness, turning it bleak, flat, ordinary and inescapable.

The more time I spent with Riparian, the less I could sit attending the tasks others deemed useful. I heard my mother's discontent and annoyance, for she blamed Riparian for this change in my nature, though she had no idea of our bond. Father stayed calm, imagining a tremendous inheritance. Nothing was done about Riparian. She remained, in daylight, tied up and removed like a bundle of laundry in her lily-white flesh, sipping Velvet Hammers in the courtyard, while at night we proceeded to meet, our alliance increasing, growing ever strong.

And then, one evening, as stories tore through me like comets, I found myself approaching Riparian's glowing centre, round and hot as molten gold, with a single fissure extending jagged like a split world.

I swam here, like a weary minnow trying to weave its way free from a fast, evaporating pool, no longer hearing Riparian's voice, nor seeing the images she projected. I swam back and forth, frantic, small, alone, and when I reached the ends of the chasm, joined the golden edges with a single nervous kiss.

Riparian sat on the bed across from me when I emerged. The sun of a new morning spilled into her room. I noticed tears of relief transforming to diamonds on her cheeks, and her broad open hands grazed my face and hair, tugging at the top of my head, pulling something free.

My skin fell away like a shroud, and I saw underneath my own electric darkness. Riparian and I walked toward the courtyard, our cloudy dimness shadowing the tumbling tea tray the housekeeper had just finished polishing.

My parents gazed in disbelief, while Riparian and I twisted day into darkness, pulled a cyclone from the earth like a snake from a basket, and made the entire subdivision of my childhood vanish forever in one breath of raucous laughter.

THE APOSTLE

Senga allowed the snake to uncoil like a gold chain around her belly. For a moment, she heard the eternal silence of death, saw its open brown mouth, its black greedy molars worn to nubs, and felt its arrow-sharp tongue. Her naked feet found the drum rhythms surely, as acknowledged wives find slippers in darkness. Her body connecting, her bones fluid fire.

Men paid money to see her dance. They sat at the edges of cabriolet chairs and teetered like divers. Some threw coins that bounced off the thick glass walls of her vivarium. But once swallowed in death's throat, Senga saw and heard nothing. It was only the pulse that touched her. Only the breath of the snake.

Other dancers veiled themselves in her shadow. It was the rancid butter she applied to calm the snake, they said, that kept her flesh so young. She came from far away, danced for many years, mothered several children whom she abandoned. But to choose a venomous cobra instead of a harmless python? That was a mystery none

could explain or understand. Even Nick, the owner of
The Viper's Pit, who needed an industrial broom to
sweep up the gratuities after Senga's performances,
couldn't understand. He'd had his lawyers draw up a
document releasing him from liability, and Senga agreed
to sign. He took a sizable cut of the money thrown by
the crowd, and knew no other dancer who could pack
the club and make him rich as she could; still he would
have paid a tidy amount himself to anyone who could
tell him why she did it.

Embraced by the snake, Senga's body moved, elastic.
Ankles, thighs, belly, midriff, breasts, encircled clock-
wise, counterclockwise, in patterns of infinity. She. Her
golden-hooded partner. Twin flames, erect, then meld-
ing. Naked limbs braiding to snake. Tongue whispering
to snake; snake woven human. It burned the eyes of
men, of jealous dancers who called her crazy and would
have done almost anything to take her place. It left a
taste in the mind, of something savoured and forgotten.

"Wasn't that something she did with that snake?" the
men muttered to each other, to Nick, to the foam of
their beer. "Whatyacallit?" The image already faded.
And so they would have to come again, see again, burn
again, forget again.

No dancer would ever follow Senga, no matter what
the terms. There was an unstated code at The Viper's
Pit, an unspoken hierarchy, with Senga always the last-
to-dance queen.

After her performance, people staggered home, chairs
were turned on table tops, Nick counted money. Senga

dressed in the bare grey light of a small changing room, then stroked her blunt-nosed partner, enjoying the ricey texture of his still warm skin before placing him into a round wicker carrier.

The streets outside glowed with flashing neon, rain puddles sparkled like road stars. Senga, now mortal in flat rubber boots, carried home her treasure, feeling his tired weight in her fingers, making her way past the junkies, the crack houses, the two overworked prostitutes at the corner who pushed hair out of each other's eyes, and the dark maroon car that slowed to pick them up. She followed the winding alley paths in darkness, feeling sound vibrate on her lips and the steady powerful wind pushing at her back. It contained the strength of her grandmother, the strength of her grandmother's grandmother, and a voice bent low to embrace both her and her partner, to cradle them.

There had been a time when Senga could not hear the voice, when she could not remember the first woman who loved her. A time when, as a small skinny child, a refugee, her mind had been wiped clean by angels, her grandmother's voice made foreign.

Yet even before she understood, the voice held her in darkness when the world disappeared; when the woman who was her mother saw dark reflections with glacial eyes, the voice wrapped her tightly in a mossy blanket and kept her warm.

And then, she touched the snake. Its body sidewinding in dusty clay, its shining ball-bearing eyes knowing and playful. She touched its small lithe head, felt her finger become its concertina, its delicate tongue lash and finally glide through her.

She was only a child, but recalls how the sky ripped open and the sun turned black, falling like a smouldering apple to the earth. How she lay suspended and paralyzed in the centre of a hurricane, her grandmother rocking at her side in a chair fashioned from oak bows, stroking snake skin, words tumbling from her wrinkled mouth like meteors, until her language was known.

"Come sit on my lap, child." The words penetrated her like a thousand tiny fangs. They shot lightning into her veins.

"You hear me now, don't you?"

She could not move, but felt her body gathered up, like water absorbed in a cloud. The fluorescent hospital lights and acrid oxygen did not welcome her. A smiling nurse patted her hand, and the scented woman who was her mother repeated, "Praise God, it's a miracle."

Plastic tubes whorled and twisted from the child's body and her weak hands made gestures to remove them.

"No!" they told her, tying her small body to the bed, taping her fingers together, securing her wrists to the metal bed frame with coarse towels.

Her throat seethed, it was as if every nerve had been scraped naked, as if every fibre of her body had become a conduit for unendurable pain. She longed only to be back where she had been, feeling the caress of the old woman's words.

"You're a wildcat," some doctor told her, "a real fighter."

She writhed and thrashed, and the woman who was her mother half closed her imploring eyes, and a nurse with a sharp silver stinger delivered liquid sleep.

The child's eyes, fierce and brown with pupils as large as moons, felt the world dissolve. Faces broke apart, words spun out of control over vast expanses of time. And the old woman, honey-coloured, knobbly-elbowed, with teeth as wide and gapped as canyons, took her onto her strong rocking lap, into her secret centre.

There, in her folds, stories and songs travelled with molten spirit. "It was a long, long, long time ago, child," her grandmother hummed, "such a long time ago, every-one wants to forget."

But the child did not forget. The child would not for-get. She would stretch her small bones wide open and drink the deep sticky nectar of the past. She would feed upon it with a hunger that had crawled and gnawed within her before she'd known life. And when finally returned to the stagnant world, to the hollow tin voices and stainless steel reflections, she would hold it all with-in her like a precious secret. Hold it there, in her own private darkness.

If anything could be done for the child, the doctor could not say what. Test after test showed nothing organically wrong. She had made a miraculous physical recovery. But afterward, there were frighteningly long periods of silence, then days and days when the child would babble, and finally seizures.

The woman who was her mother locked the child in the hall closet, her hands trembling as she turned the key. At times she thought it was Satan who had come upon the child. Satan in the guise of a snake, just as he had arrived in the Garden of Eden, and she begged the minister of her church to intervene.

But the minister prided himself in being level-headed. It could not be Satan, he told the woman. "Why should Satan strike your child? You? When there are so many others to take who don't have recourse to God?"

The child was examined by neurological specialists, seen by psychiatrists. She was asked to play in sandboxes with little plastic toys, draw pictures with bright magic markers, recite dreams, but it was always the snake: the snake, as big as the biggest buildings; the ghost snake no one but she saw; the snake who slept under her pillow, hid between the walls of her house; the snake who lived everywhere.

The seizures worsened and could not be predicted. The child could not go to school like an ordinary child. She could not do simple things.

Sometimes she stood in the centre of the treeless fenced yard hissing until the woman who was her mother had to drag her away. It was humiliating, terrifying, yet the woman knew she could not blame the child.

And then the woman was told about a special place, a school where the child would be kept clean and fed. And on holidays, the woman could visit. She could bring boxes of chocolates, birthday cakes, and sweaters; she could go there first, before she made any decisions, inspect the grounds, see for herself the beautiful gardens, speak to the staff.

Here, the child fell most deeply into the folds of her grandmother's skirt. Days and nights of induced sleep converged and no words hindered.

"They want you to forget, child," her grandmother rasped, "just like they all, but baby child, you hang on."

She wrapped the child in an old clear snake skin, the outline of folds and milky triangular scales obscuring vision. With a long claw needle she sutured.

"This'll keep'em out," she hummed, "this ole skin'll keep you safe till you ready to bust free."

And for years the child became invisible, strapped to a hollow metal bed frame in the institution, eyes unblinking, as her soul travelled in the grandmother's world.

It was the grandmother who named her Senga, the grandmother who taught her to dance with snakes.

"You gotta make the connection right, honey. Feel the roots of your feet. Dig 'em in deep enough, so nothin' can move you." The snake skulls strung around the old woman's neck shook and grinned. Fire flared in their empty sockets. "You got it, baby. You got the gift."

Contained in the warmth of the grandmother's world, Senga learned to see and listen. The palms of her hands tingled with the smallest movements, her breath absorbed images, her flesh heard. She learned to trust the snakes. To let them roam her body, explore her mind, fill her with their golden wild fire.

"Everyone's wantin' to forget where they come from," the old woman murmured. "Everyone likes to pretend there ain't no startin' place. But you, honey, you gonna take that gift back and remind 'em in time."

So Senga danced like a fuse. She danced like a beacon. Her body substanceless light, able to shine and
cast shadow, able to bring vision as well as blind. She
danced and experienced her self becoming, her child
body stretching, filling with wakefulness, the flare of
her brilliance, the heat of her kinesis, setting the world
ablaze.

It was thought to have begun in an antiquated boiler
room in the basement. Hundreds perished trying to
escape. But Senga slid from the sleep of her grandmother's world, crawled across the melting tile floor of the
institution, slithered through flames. Her skin smoking
and smouldering, steaming like volcanic pools.

The steely door was not bolted in the wing where her
bed blistered, where sightless women and voiceless girls
writhed in the ashes of their own flesh. The back draft
scoured the walls clean of paint, licked innards out,
scattered charred teeth like dice, until the hazy, guiltless
morning when the fire was extinguished.

Few bodies were recovered. Most disappeared as completely as if they had never existed. The child was
thought to be among them, but Senga had made her
escape. She crawled out into the surrounding parkland
and covered herself with the healing chill of earth. She
slept beneath a large grey oak, its empty twining
branches providing shelter. And when she woke, she
knew she glistened. The old skin of the grandmother lay
heaped at her naked feet.

She would not go back to the grandmother's world
now, but would receive messages. There were things to

be had on the slick black streets: food and clothing, sex and money. Even the cobra, she found there. He had been smuggled from another country as a conversation piece, used to kill a junkie who could not pay what he owed, then abandoned.

The grandmother always spoke to her, always reminded her, "Everyone lives right next door to death, child. Trouble is most don't take the time to get even a little bit acquainted till they gotta be roommates."

And as Senga ascended the crumbling stairs of the chalky building where she rented a room, she heard the grandmother whisper now and knew it would not be long before the world remembered.

Her partner licked the air, his tongue penetrating worn wicker slats, his lungs expanding to hear the old woman's vibrations.

"Ssssssenga," he whispered, eager to curve into her warm body, "Ssssenga."

The room was dark and chilly. Senga freed her partner, kissed his smooth head, then fed him fresh rats and roaches enticed out of walls.

When he was full, he twisted over her like a vine, his tongue smelling her skin, full of music.

He wanted to know something. He wanted to know. So he wriggled up her arm, perched on her shoulder, under her hair. He melted into the nape of her neck like a lover, wrapped his body once around her waist. The grandmother's breath rattled and penetrated the small square window. Dashes of rain like splinters of broken glass chipped the cold linoleum floor. The smell of wet smoke drizzled a fine mist like a graceful genie, and the snake whispered, "What will happen? When they remember, what will happen to us?"

The lobe of Senga's ear quivered like a taut string. "Rest," she told him, "don't worry now."

DRYING THE BONES

Auntie's house stood above water. A steep, scraggy moment, tasting of eternity to some, with giant ivory pillars that curved and pointed like elephant tusks and ill-hinged doors that swung perpendicular. Bobbinet lace curtains, twisting to nooses, fluttered like unravelling wings at the windows, spilling past sepia shades and peeling sills, down broken cinder trellises where white morning-glories ascended to sun.

For a time, I lived here, ensconced. The walls' damp shadows my playmates, the mute wood floors my confidants. I sailed through Auntie's house a vagrant traveller, my heart suspended, my feet only touching air, and Auntie's voice all alive in my mind's fire, burning.

Before she had come for me, I did not know her in any way. Her great chrome face a mystery, the darkest ravine. And then the day arrived, her long black car gleaming silver beside the fields, and mamma crying and wringing her hands, and telling me to lie low and quiet until she passed.

The soft moist earth absorbed my back and legs, and the shimmering sugar cane danced over me, its violet stalks beyond my reach, its massive leaves spinning and jousting like swords. I lay with my heart digging the earth, my hands empty, listening, and mamma kneeling beside me whispering charms.

I remember thinking I could lie here forever, light and shadow sprinkling my face, a ripe young seed embraced in the slippery soil with mamma above me keeping me safe. And then, I was sleeping, and the world was gone. And when I awoke, I was with Auntie, and the opaque evening dust, rolling us through streets, away from everything and everyone I had ever known, and Auntie touching me, with long slender fingers inside fine white gloves smelling of lavender. Her luminous black car streaking the horizon like ink.

She told me I was hungry and gave me apples. Crisp sweet apples with icy skins and flesh that filled my mouth and belly. Her body was warm, its heat infused me, and I moved closer, my damp leg touching her satiny thigh, my hair brushing her shoulder.

Her lean arm encircled me, drawing me closer still into her soft dark curves, until I could no longer tell where she began or I ended, and soon, anaesthetized by lavender, could no longer care.

The road behind us seemed to collapse upon itself and disappear until darkness erased it, while the yearning car moved always faster, consuming powdery black miles.

At the ends of the earth, there was water. Grey-green incandescent water, quivering and flashing a million gold minnows, and a large austere boat, larger than seven mansions, carrying me and Auntie away.

For days there was nothing but sheets of water, billowing and pitching or lying flat as coin, and the sun and moon, a beam balance scale suspended by pulleys.

Most nights I cried for mamma, feeling sick, cuddling down in my berth, thinking how she loved me, and Auntie would let me cry, saying it was best. When I'd settled down, she'd take my hand, lead me on deck, point to the constellations in heaven and my wet eyes would catch their wonder and I'd begin to see the world afresh.

"Everything changes," Auntie would tell me. She'd look out at the darkness as if she saw faces there, and then she'd lead me back to our cabin, and I'd lay my head on the salty pillow and she'd stay with me until I slept.

Sometimes when I felt bold, I would ask her if I would ever see mamma again, and her ruby lips would twist into a high smile, a tapered finger turning a curl on the top of my head as she sighed, and then I would feel sad for her, because she had been kind and it seemed she wished I could forget. But even after I had lived in her house for many years, had learned what was expected and no longer felt anything, I still could not forget completely all she wished me to, although my memory, like the bright gay flowered walls in the little room where I slept, did begin to dim, and the gifts she showered upon me grew tiresome.

The fine embroidered dresses and long white stockings, which at first made me feel a princess, came in time to represent my captivity, and all the cheerful coloured toys festooning her dreary house were nothing more than attractive links of my unassailable gilded chain.

It began as a game, sweet and magical, with Auntie the fairy queen, delivering me to extraordinary destinies. Sometimes I pretended she was my mother, that I would grow to resemble her, and she enjoyed hearing these fantasies and encouraged me in their elaboration.

She'd give me small tokens of approval from her jewellery case, rhinestone brooches with pins as sharp as silver darts and strings of imitation pearls knotted at my chest, clattering like dry bones. Sometimes she would sit me down before her large oval mirror, rouge my cheeks and paint my lips until they glowed and I no longer recognized myself, and then she would declare me beautiful.

Elderly men would call, huffing and puffing up the winding path like small withered leaves propelled by sudden gusts of wind, and for a time I enjoyed watching them arrive, their wet eyes bright, their intimate smiles.

Auntie swung her long hair loose from its twining braid, instructing me to play in my room, but I would stand outside her parlour door, listening to the grunts and wheezes and the limping commands of her guests, wondering what it was that occupied them.

In time, I was invited in and asked to sit on the spiky laps of old gentlemen, whose pink spotted hands reminded me of spiders, and whose faces hung like ancient cloth awnings over empty windows.

At night, I shivered under musty blankets, while frightening images danced and mocked me from the pitch black walls, and the room inched in, a living corset, constricting my movements, consuming my breath.

I saw the tall scarlet fields I could not forget, the hazy nights flickering to morning, and then I saw mamma moving through winding lanes, her shawl slapping her shoulders as she searched, calling me, and I sobbed for her until she turned and I awoke suddenly, chilled and alone.

Afterwards, I could not go into Auntie's parlour. It was as if a wall had been erected at the threshold that stopped my obedient feet and legs, and weakened my anxious stomach. Instead, I swept moldy fetid floors and cleaned the black oven where I imagined the souls of wrinkled old men had been burned, and I buffed the mahogany stair railings and scrubbed every square inch of wood till the skin peeled off the tips of my fingers and grew back as smooth and hard as polished stone.

Auntie fed me in exchange for my work, but the meals were meagre and few, served up with cruel reproofs and the promise things would remain as they were until I had learned to be less proud. The beautiful embroidered dresses all dissolved to threads, the white stockings to nothingness, the colourful toys all vanished, and I was moved from my elegant room to a small grey one beneath the stairs that was dark and drafty and full of decay. In the end, there was nothing of the former magic, yet I remained held fast, while Auntie, my persuasive captor, kept me weak with hunger and exhausted from work.

At times, she still spoke to me in kindly tones, asking me to come to her parlour and play. But I could not tell her that it was my mamma who forbade me the game, that as we spoke, she searched for me and wept, and that I knew in my heart she would not rest until I had been found.

My silence infuriated Auntie. She considered me ungrateful and moved toward the steaming hearth of her parlour, a blazing star. I felt so suddenly her warmth evaporate. It was as if the blood in my veins would freeze, but then I would think of mamma searching in the fields and realize that to desire Auntie's brilliant light was betrayal.

I stood on the platform of the grey balcony, which woodworms slowly consumed, beating thick dusty carpets over the balustrade. Clouds grew before me, blinding waves of smoke, and when they cleared, in the distance, I saw her. A young girl, no older than myself, strolling up the crooked hedged path as if dazed.

Her hair was long and fine, the colour of a ripe peach, her face, narrow and bloodless. As she came closer, I noticed the delicacy of her facial features; in fact, the whole of her looked carved from wax. I wanted to shout to her, tell her not to come to this evil house, but the words strained painfully in my throat, choking me before ever they could form, and her swaying body moved, a curling piece of shaved steel toward a most powerful magnet.

I imagined her pallid hand extending as she reached for the tarnished brass lion knocker, whose teeth and mane looked all the more vicious for the stains of age that polish could not erase; and then I saw Auntie, sailing through the musty grandeur of bygone years, clipping the air with haste, her eyes cast forward.

The door opened in anticipation. Auntie's soothing voice spoke. There was an inchoate murmur from the stranger, and the door shut fast. I watched from the balcony to see if the stranger would leave, but she did not appear again, and I began to doubt myself.

Not too long afterward, one of Auntie's gentlemen arrived, and I heard the hollow heels of her shoes clattering as she led him to her parlour, the softness of her contrived mood. I knew she would come looking for me soon, looking to see that I'd done all I was meant to and to set more tasks, and so I pushed my old polishing rag into the crevices of the balcony door and continued with my work.

Behind Auntie's door, there were deep-toned chuckles, insincere praise, and the stringy chords of ancient gentlemen visitors, whose voices reverberated in every interstice of Auntie's dwelling.

Sometimes, I could not bear them, my legs turning limp, my stomach churning at their sounds. I covered my ears as if I were snuffing small fires. Still, I heard them echo.

The hallways of Auntie's house were long and angular, never quite the same from one day to the next, and often, it seemed, when gentleman left her parlour they became hopelessly lost.

As I polished, I imagined the many unfound. Men who had petrified, sinking back into panelled wood, becoming shadows, and I spat on my duster and swore at the knots till they glistened.

I moved from corridors to the kitchen, down steep, hidden stairs, where fleets of servants' feet had once ascended, the wood weathered, the banister frail.

The kitchen itself, a mammoth structure with jagged walls rising twenty feet to sloping ceilings, remained inhabited by spirits of the past. There were large copper vessels and pipes, all green now. I approached the fireplace with a hot steel bucket and brush, and on swollen knees scrubbed the charred stones, moving backward and forward in a steady hypnotic motion. In the moment that my eyes closed, I saw mamma, clearly moving through cane, shaking her frantic fists, swinging her hips, screaming.

Something stirred in the crusty cinder before me, bringing me back. A mouse or rat, I thought, tearing across stone, but then I saw her, the girl, looking paler than a slaughtered hen. She touched me and I could smell the clean sweet air of home, feel the earth's moist embrace.

Her name was Bianca, she said. She had come from the village to work for the woman. Her family was poor. While she spoke, I was aware of her vague mesmerizing tone, reminding me of songs I had heard long ago but could not fully recall, and at last I was convinced mamma had somehow sent her.

She disappeared into a stream of dusty light—rogue, invasive, sliding into the kitchen from a high round window that could not be shaded. Then I heard the sound of Auntie's heels tapping like dissatisfied bones on the stairs and struggled to continue scrubbing layers of darkness away as if nothing had occurred.

The winter came and went with glacial moon-swept skies and the murder of newborn life, and Auntie's house, chilled to the heart, continued standing, a pre-historic reptile whose blood had frozen almost solid.

Old men trudged the slick diamond path to Auntie's house; Arctic explorers they seemed, with boots and over-coats so heavy they bent bones like wire hangers, and the world continued for a time preserved, suspended. The water that crawled beneath us moved with arthritic pre-cision, mirrored oppressive clouds and swallowed drops of daylight. Bianca vanished, a petal under ice, and did not appear again until after the thaw when the days began to stretch themselves forward into starry evenings, and the shroud of frost dropped from the planet.

During the cold months, I doubted and searched. My old room, with its brown blossomed wallpaper now peeling, remained empty, and nowhere I examined showed signs of her young life. Somewhere, I imagined, locked away with toys and trinkets, the lonely girl waited, and my nights became restless and tormented as I roamed the sleeping house with anxious dreams.

Then, the spring came, and the stagnant silence that had held the house broke. Auntie's voice was suddenly everywhere, and beneath it, pinned to its will, those familiar inflections of Bianca's that had stirred my memory when first I'd heard them and now gave me cause for the greatest hope.

I scrubbed floors and smoky hearthstones with renewed vigour, allowing myself always to move deeply into the rhythm of the task and open myself to whatever visions might arrive, knowing before long I would see her again.

And then, one afternoon, she did arrive, dressed in a velvet embroidered jumper of the kind I once wore. White stockings decorated her long childish legs, and she lifted a finger to her lips, so I knew we must meet in silence. Still, it was as if she whispered constantly to me about the woman who kept her locked away in a room at the other end of the sprawling house and fed her with candies and sweet cakes and gave her many beautiful things to play with and wear.

The woman, she whispered, whose face shone silver, possessed many voices, her skin many variations. She moved sometimes without her body, sometimes with the body of others. All these things Bianca whispered to me without words.

I wanted to ask her if she knew my mamma, if she had been sent to this house in order to free me, but we heard Auntie, the sound of her breath penetrating walls, and Bianca vanished noiselessly.

Auntie's teeth dominated her face. They glistened like rows of sparkling windows, while her eyes were almost absent. I bowed my head, averted my own gaze, as I felt her laser perception slicing deep into my thoughts.

"No, I've seen no one. I've heard nothing." It was a robotic voice inside me that spoke, yet it satisfied Auntie, who turned on her heels and drifted away.

The familiar brocade rugs and the time-worn scent of hoary gentlemen made me dizzy and forgetful, yet I recalled now the large black book, encased in glass in

Auntie's parlour. The book, she once said, she cherished above all things. It contained the history of her family, and when first I came to live with her, she added my name to its yellowing ledger.

Bianca howled through the chimney that this book must be destroyed; she chanted through the seething kettle, and I listened, quaking, certain that Auntie would return. My hand extended toward her but felt only darkness. There was no light, and her small childish body pushed against me urgently.

She created a poppet from kitchen sweepings, insisting I always carry it hidden, and in the blackest moments of night she led me through secret passageways, behind walls, and up stairways I had never seen, bringing me finally to Auntie's parlour.

I felt the solid bureau and knew it would support me as I retrieved the book from its glass case secured so high upon the wall. Bianca's face was ghostly, her body like a white taper, yet she smiled when we held the heavy volume together and even seemed to gain strength. We fed the devouring fire in the kitchen with torn pages, Bianca dancing in circles as I searched the flames for signs. Suffering charred faces hid behind comburent light, and for a moment, I heard them scream, and saw a flaming scythe mowing them away. In the searing smoke there were slender rods of cane growing high into magenta canopies, and in the slow-burning embers, there was mamma, nodding her head.

I woke the following morning, cold and drenched with sweat, wondering what awaited me. I called for

Bianca, hoping she would stand beside me now, as I feared the wrath of Auntie more than I feared anything, but Bianca did not arrive, and I scrambled to the kitchen, clutching the poppet Bianca had made for me, in order to begin the daily round of chores as if nothing had occurred.

It was not until late afternoon that I heard the sour groan of Auntie's parlour door push open, and felt her invasive shadow slide over me like a noose. I crouched in the hallway, shoving my ragged duster against the distended skirting board, preparing my body and mind for the blow I was certain would follow. But Auntie glided past as if in a trance. She did not acknowledge my presence in any way; in fact, her complete lack of attention made me wonder if I were truly still alive.

My eyes followed her down swelling halls. She limped slightly, as if one tired heel had finally fallen asleep and her thin legs were not up to supporting her. And there was something else also, something I could not immediately see but only considered afterwards. Her face and flesh had begun to lose their sheen, and the dazzling, overpowering light she emitted had already begun to dim.

Each passing day absorbed her brightness, until she no longer had the energy for fury, only apprehension. I boldly pushed my ear against the door of her parlour now, listening to her sob, knowing that her body was failing, and I summoned Bianca who listened with me; our joint effort had vanquished her, and together we revelled in our success.

I continued waxing and buffing the expanse of pock-marked wood in the house; I continued polishing and shining, sweeping and beating, scrubbing so meticulously that inflamed, wet blisters rose on my knuckles, even over the calluses, and I laughed when I heard Auntie cry.

Old gentlemen scaled the steep path to her house steaming with frantic hearts, yet the door remained shut. Auntie locked her parlour and would see no one.

Evidence of Auntie's nightly sojourns soon became visible: a woody black toe unconsciously abandoned, a derelict finger pointing south. Bianca would shriek and clap her hands as I examined these finds, so decayed and shrunken as to be almost unrecognizable, but we knew what they were and collected them scrupulously, for we also knew their power.

By firelight we sewed small cotton squares together with drawstring ties to contain these relics, and then we hung them about my body, under my clothes, close to the poppet Bianca had made, in order to keep us safe from harm.

Mamma rocked back and forth, her knees pressed flat to her chest, staring out at me, proud, from the bright flames. Then she was telling us what to do, talking just as I remembered.

I took Auntie a tray in the morning—thin coffee and dry toast, as mamma had told me—and opened the door to her parlour without waiting for her to say I could. She was there on the day bed, skinny and bent as a wire, pulling handfuls of sheets to her face to hide its erosion.

I didn't bow my head when I saw her because I was

no longer afraid, even though her voice, when she tried to speak, was thick and breathless.

She was asking me to bring a doctor to the house, although all she had the strength to say was the single word, and I stood there watching until her hands let loose the dirty sheets.

I moved closer then, listening to her rasp, watching her eyes flicker, and I stayed for a long while because I knew it would be the last time.

Bianca and I found half a dozen planks in the cellar covered in cobwebs and mouse droppings. Together we dragged them up the stairs, and with a handful of steel nails and a heavy rock, hammered them across Auntie's parlour door. Then, we stood there, waiting to hear Auntie make some kind of a cry or a moan, anything to let us know she realized what had happened. But no sound came.

All night long, we stirred bleeding embers of fire, and told mamma what we'd done and talked about the way it used to be. And when daylight finally started to cover the stony kitchen floor with its pale tongue, and we could no longer hold the fire and Bianca disappeared like a wax candle, I filled my steel bucket with boiling water and began scouring.

I worked like a demon all morning, mopping and swabbing the filthy rooms of Auntie's house, flushing and rinsing, till I could see my own bones glowing slick, and when I came to the parlour door, I stopped to lean against it, remembering the feel of earth on my back, lost in my first embrace.

THE OVERSEER

Mama Cassava's plywood lean-to sat smack in the middle of everywhere, nestled between two tall government buildings with tops so high and sharp they almost cut the moon.

"You be careful up there," Mama Cassava shouted to the buildings, "don't you go choppin' apart somethin' you got no right to touch." She swept the alleyway with stiff rags and newspapers tied together on the broken branch of one of those potted trees you see lining the street in front of shopping malls.

Sometimes over the din of honking horns and police sirens, she heard her broom talking. Right now, it was saying, "sweep clean, sweep clean," and it was piling up small brown-glass gems made out of beer bottles, crinkly see-through paper, cigarette butts, and the soulless dusty footprints of big wing-tipped shoes.

Most people walking past barely noticed her muttering to her talking broom and shouting at the buildings, who obediently pulled back whenever she told them off.

Fewer still noticed the little grey cardboard sign swinging outside her place announcing her business.

But every now and again, some civil servant from one of the big buildings next door, or some desperado, or some searching soul, would shortcut through the alley, see her sign, and get curious, for Mama Cassava dealt in futures.

She had an old deck of mismatched playing cards, and a lively candle made from a tin can and creosote rags, whose flame never expired. She'd set the cards down on a cardboard box anyway they chose to be set, and she'd rock back on an old wooden orange crate, "Uuuunnhuh, mmmmm," she'd listen to what the cards had to tell her, and then she'd talk.

"Don't you try foolin' yourself into believin' you got a right, you're bein' unfaithful to a good woman," she'd say, or "You been stealin' money from where you work, you gotta come clean, and make it up." Mama Cassava didn't hold with pussyfooting. "You're as selfish as a shellfish," she'd shout. It didn't matter to Mama Cassava that the enquirer went all red, squirmed around like a worm at the end of a hook and vanished into the night without so much as a thank you. Sometimes people needed a powerful dose of truth to kick start them in the direction of the future, and she knew that was why they'd ended up coming to her.

Along with doses of truth, Mama Cassava sometimes prescribed special medicines she'd made herself, consisting of anything from alley sweepings to plants she'd come across in parks, to government documents she'd rescued from sanitation bins, to the fur, fangs and fleas of stray dogs and cats, who usually came bearing important information, or occasionally just for a friendly chat.

"You take this, sweet pea," she'd say to young women who arrived in terrible straits, handing them little clumps of wilty green leaves. "You forget all about that old coat hanger notion. Mama Cassava ain't gonna let you die."

And the young women would kiss the raggedy fringes at the bottom of the old lady's skirt. But Mama Cassava didn't concern herself much with gratitude. "You get up now," she'd say, "you got a future waitin' on you."

Mama Cassava was rarely anxious, rarely worried, but lately she swept the alleyway late, late into the night, with one eye on the moon and the other on those mischievous government buildings, asking her broom, "Who's gonna take care of things when I'm gone?"

The broom didn't like the thought of her not being around, so it only said, "sweep clean," and tried to get her talking on another subject.

It seemed to Mama Cassava, especially over the past few years, there'd been too much traffic through the alleyway, and lately, she'd been seeing troubles she'd never had to put right before. She was getting more and more people coming to her whose futures had been snuffed before they'd started living. Children who'd been abandoned by young women who hadn't found their way to Mama Cassava in time, teenage drug addicts with needle death sentences, and adults with their hearts torn right out, numb to the touch of truth—vacant and futureless.

Mama Cassava was getting tired looking for medicines that seemed to be increasingly in short supply, except for the alley sweepings, which were always plentiful but not always of good quality, and her cards were getting frayed around the edges and tired too. But most threatening were the government buildings, which had begun to multiply and were starting to get uppity and hard to keep in line. There were five or six of them now, and they laughed and swayed and jousted with one another, and intimidated the moon with their sabre-sharp points. "I'm warnin' you," Mama Cassava shouted, her voice still strong, though a little scratchy and weary, "you settle down up there, or you'll be wishin' you never got built."

Her threats meant less and less to them. They mocked her with an echo. "Never got built, never got built, never," they said and poked at the moon.

Mama Cassava couldn't let them out of her sight for a second, and alley traffic was getting hectic. Every morning now there were crushed and empty-looking people waiting outside her lean-to. Sometimes there were lines that stretched all the way back to the housing projects.

When Scrawny, the tabby, came hunting for her, he could barely get through. Mama Cassava had pulled her orange crate chair, table box, and creosote rag candle outside her lean-to and was setting card after tired card out in front of her as she kept vigil over the government buildings.

"I'm too busy to visit," she told the tabby, setting down the next six cards and hunting in her shabby empty pocket for some medicine she thought she might still have a sprinkling of.

The tabby wound himself around her ankles, then jumped up on her lap and shinnied up her hunched shoulders. He had to nibble at her ear before he got her attention, but finally she folded up her cards and listened.

It seemed the birds had overheard the government buildings talking. The buildings declared war on the moon. "Sharp, reckless, useless," the buildings chanted, "cut her to ribbons tonight."

Mama Cassava shook her head. "You'd think something so lofty would know better," she told the cat, and turned over the fluttering little cardboard sign hanging on her lean-to. She would be doing no more business today.

The people lining the alley moved on. Those who had homes went there; those who didn't went back to the park. A nervous silence screamed through the middle of everywhere. Mama Cassava's broom twitched with terror.

"Uuuhuh, mmmm," Mama Cassava said, gazing into the growing blue centre of the flame of her candle. "Them buildings got to be stopped." But strangers carrying briefcases passing by the street in front of her alley didn't hear a word. And when Mama Cassava took to those same streets, shouting and mumbling, carrying her candle in one hand and waving the other in a fist, no one would meet her eye; it was as if she'd become invisible. Even the government buildings stood up straight at first, whistled and pretended not to see her.

"I know what you got up your sleeves," she shouted at them. "I know what you're all up to."

A couple of buildings jumped, another couple pulled back. She smashed their windows with her bare fists. "Cut her to ribbons," they called, "cut her to ribbons."

Blood trickled down Mama Cassava's arms into the tin can of her candle and was sucked right up by the creosote rags. The flame skipped and danced and jumped through the windows, tickling curtains and walls with fingers as bright as the moon.

"Stop," the buildings shrieked, "Oh, please, stop, you're cracking us up!" And the nimble fiery fingers showed no mercy, but proceeded travelling to the most sensitive spots that the buildings squirmed desperately to conceal.

By dawn, the fire was extinguished. Mama Cassava stood in the centre of the smoking ruins. An ambulance took her to a hospital. Her arms were bandaged so she couldn't move them, and she was laced down to a bed in a room that locked from the outside. Through the room's barred windows she could only watch the city and see the government buildings growing back like warts.

"You gotta watch them buildings," she called to the nurses. "Them buildings want to cut apart the moon."

Madonna Rosa

When the snow brought its dusty morning, covering street lamps and traffic signals in a chilly luminous screen, Madonna Rosa looked beyond the square window frame of her mountain dwelling and saw she must travel to the city.

"Good-bye, my dears," she whispered, her tears creating mud as they washed down her sagging face, collected in wrinkles, puddled in the concentric grooves of her collar bone. Her wooden chair and table rattled, her black-bellied pot tipped its lid. Even the mossy floor, always so placid beneath her, heaved with verdant grief.

The summer before last, she had collected coarse goat's fleece that clung to the brambles like swaying cocoons and woven herself a fine, shaggy blanket. Now it stretched out before her, an invitation to serve, so she filled it with sturdy red branches of mahogany, her tip-bent knife, and an old tarnished locket someone once had given her in payment for prayers.

With the soles of her broad dark feet tougher than

rawhide and her legs slightly bowed, she ambled down the mountainside, coming in time to the dazzling city that sprawled before her.

Automobiles crawled through swelling white streets, hurrying pedestrians braced themselves and bent toward slippery cold pavements. Madonna Rosa stood for a moment like a frozen tree, drinking in these busy spectacles, then turned open-faced to the sky, for it was there, she knew, she would find what she needed.

A black crow, gliding like a feathered arrow, led Madonna Rosa to the centre of the city. Stately buildings, full of self-importance, surrounded her, and she dropped her goat's fleece bundle where she stopped, beside a sanitation bin under the sagging canopy of a small, neglected shop.

Boards barred the windows and doorway, sharp splinters of glass sprinkled the snow. Madonna Rosa extended her palm, holding it for a moment like a level in the air, as wind embroidered her fingers.

Under the snow and glass, her hand burrowed, finding at last a wooden stake as stiff and strong as moonshine and a stone as smooth as gold. Using these tools, she freed the plywood barricade at the shop's door and entered the building as if it were her accustomed way.

All around was crumbling and littered. Cobwebs dangled like rope nets from the ceilings. Broken bottles, brick, bloated plasterboard, all mingled in a visual cacophony of ruin.

Madonna Rosa collected sheets of discarded newspaper that curled against the walls like carpets, tore them into strips, tied them with old shoe string, and joined them to a branch that fell from her bundle. She swept the shop from floor to ceiling, accumulating mounds of debris and salvaging limping spiders that crawled to her hands for comfort.

Outside, the wind howled. Madonna Rosa stacked the contents of her bundle in a corner, smoothed her goat's fleece blanket on the floor and rested awhile as the night unrolled its dark cape the length of the city.

Street noises serenaded Madonna Rosa as she slept, filling her dreams with the most exotic movements: simple mountain birds no longer chirped but squealed and honked, black bears shrieked drunken obscenities, then exploded into swelling clouds.

Madonna Rosa trudged down from the mountain again and again, coming to the abandoned shop, making of it a humble resting place, planting in the earth around her legions of shining seeds that dropped from her ragged pockets as if she herself were a tree.

In the morning when she woke, warm sun spilled through the splintering cracks of the boarded shop windows. The wind relinquished its grief. The world beyond her dripped its thawing icicles, and Madonna Rosa stood and nodded, for she had summoned spring.

She set a crate outside the store front to sit upon, brought some wood and her tip-bent knife, and whittled as she watched thin veils of ice transform to water at her feet.

People bustled by scarcely seeing, but Madonna Rosa continued carving. Often she chattered to herself, to the objects of her creation, and occasionally, lifting her wide toothless mouth, greeted passing strangers as if they were old friends.

Her hands concealed the tiny creatures as she freed them from wood. Birds of all description, white-tailed deer, coons and cougars flourished, surrounding her and her lopsided crate.

Each day she resumed, and the days grew increasingly bright. Snow melted to reveal apartment window boxes dense with the promise of tulips, and fanning malls announced the winter's end with banners longer than city blocks.

Evenings, Madonna Rosa stood and stretched her thick, gnarled fingers, ordered her multiplying menagerie to stand guard, and paced the city streets in search of food. She ate scraps in old twisted lunch bags and retrieved cartons from city bins. Fast food alley offerings of burgers and fries she gathered like blackberries into her skirt and carried back to the thin rodents who shared her city dwelling.

The selfless wooden beasts that Madonna Rosa had brought into being never partook of her gifts, no matter how she enticed them. They guarded the shop like a host of chiselled angels, daring only the occasional movement, which Madonna Rosa caught with her sharp eyes. At night, when Madonna Rosa's dreams revealed all possibilities, they crawled and leapt and cantered in the folds of her skirt, foraged under her elbows' knobbly curves, soared past her sleeping head. By morning, the whole of her tingled and shone from spinning hooves.

Her coarse hair twisted and coiled like snakes. The beasts resumed their solid vigil, and Madonna Rosa shrieked, delighted with their ability to play.

As spring opened to summer and days became longer than nights, tourists with wallets bulging in their pockets began to traverse the thoroughfare where Madonna Rosa made her home, and few could resist stopping and offering money for her tiny creations.

"Such charming little carvings," they would say, "and what an eccentric old woman."

But when Madonna Rosa smiled her shameless smile and shook her ancient head refusing to part with her treasures, then the tourists called her "crazy" and pulled their children away from her menagerie.

Madonna Rosa's knife blade clicked. She hummed and laughed and spoke to herself, and rocked back and forth on her crate.

Tourists crawled back to hotel rooms. People who worked in the city by day slunk sleepily home to their beds. The flaming moon rose and danced in the sky like a gypsy, and then Madonna Rosa took to the streets.

Stray dogs and cats escorted her, the starry night unrolled a glittering path. Madonna Rosa took only what was meant for her, then ambled back to her broken-down shop, preparing herself for a night of visions.

And then one night, as her playful beasts frolicked in and on the creases of her dreams, a hunter came in a red plaid shirt with a gun swinging at his side.

"Go away," Madonna Rosa told him, "the beasts are not for sale." Her toothless mouth turned slack, her cheerful eyes filled with poison, and when the hunter refused to leave, pointing his gun toward her skittering beasts, Madonna Rosa leapt at him, her brittle nails extended.

The following morning went poorly for Madonna Rosa. The branches she tried to carve split and cracked like worn seams and disgruntled tourists commented unkindly.

"Crazy old bitch ought to be locked away."

The wooden animals subdued their growls, Madonna Rosa dragged her swaying crate indoors, and the rats and mice sniffed the sombre air and fled as if they sensed a natural disaster.

Madonna Rosa bent and shook her worried head. "The hunter," she muttered, grabbing the objects of her creation, pushing them into any crumbling plaster holes or apertures she could find. On the dusty floor, she wrapped herself tightly in her blanket, pulling the covers under and in, creating a soft pouch where she could remain invisible. Yet, in sleep, the hunter found her again and again, at first arriving alone through swelling thickets of sound, then gradually, increasing his number as Madonna Rosa struggled against him.

Armies of plaid-coated hunters stormed Madonna Rosa's shop, kicking in wooden barricades, knocking through brick. The small beasts huddled and shivered in frozen hiding places while Madonna Rosa fought valiantly with her tip-bent knife.

For seven days Madonna Rosa continued to resist— her weak, emaciated body growing feverishly hot as she sliced at hunters, who dropped in and out of her dreams like dangerous comets.

And then, on the eighth day, a tourist walking past her shop overheard the muffled screams. Police and paramedics were summoned, and Madonna Rosa found and taken away.

"But the animals," she cried, clutching the sleeves of the men who hoped to save her, trying in vain to find her little treasures in the folds of her skirt.

She could make no one understand. Dry tears stuck in her eyes. A needle was inserted in her hand, fluid pushed through her parched body.

"The hunters will kill them," she told the nurses and doctors, and she struggled against them to be free.

They took her knife, put her in a locked room, forced drugs and tubes into her body, but she continued to wail and fight, for she could not ignore the frightened beasts so far from her, who still cried loudly in despair.

"Don't you hear?" she asked the shadows on her wall, but the shadows stood mute, as the cries of her animals seemed to fill the world with grief.

After some time, when Madonna Rosa no longer wept and her mind was numb with medicine, she was allowed to walk the corridors of the hospital in her long blue robe and paper slippers.

She heard the cries still—coldly distant, frightened, disengaged—as doctors and nurses nodded, as patients writhed in the night, as the world turned a somersault and leaves as dead as bone tapped caged windows like metronomes. Pelting rain dug holes in the earth, filled stifled troughs, overflowed into fields once scorched by summer. And brightly charged hospital hallways hummed with artificial light.

In the lounge, tables overflowed with bounty for the psychiatric patients: fresh-cut sandwiches, muffins, scones, none of which Madonna Rosa took.

She walked slowly in circles, paced and swayed in alternating designs, and soon the others knew who she was, followed in her path, and called for her healing.

Sounds bubbled and churned in her throat, her limp hands fell upon the heads and shoulders of those who reached to touch her gown, absorbing their suffering as a shield, yet still the hunters stalked.

"Go away," Madonna Rosa screamed, and needles swiftly jabbed her veins, dimness gave way to dark, and hunters—swarms and swarms of hunters—crawled down from porous ceilings, trampling her helpless body and wounding her flesh.

The doctors and nurses could not see the bullet holes where rusty streams of blood began. They could not understand her wild, raging terror, her obscene, aching groans. Other patients crowded outside, watching the stain of her blood seep beyond the door of her room and wash down the corridor.

"Save her!" one woman demanded, and then the others demanded also and shouted and thumped at her locked door until all the hospital security staff assembled.

Madonna Rosa bled, and the blood covered the floor, splashing high on the walls, oozing through window cracks and dripping off bars.

Her body was dropping away, turning liquid, and her mind closing. The persistent thumping outside the locked door, which she comprehended only vaguely at first, now filled her soul with a burst of sudden joy. The snorting and growling and cawing, the swelling dust, beating life open, released her stampede of wooden animals, who roared into her room in a cloud of dancing thunder.

They nuzzled and licked her dry aching face, leapt happily into the purple folds of her blood-soaked gown. Wasting no time Madonna Rosa gathered them up in her arms, discarded her failing body, and scaled the mountain she had come from almost a year before.

THE VILLA

The path wound like an untidy skein through the village, around outlining woods, and up, far up, into the balding hill where the sun spilled sweet liqueur in small certain portions, warming us as we laboured in the fields.

My sister and I, tumbling together in heaps of straw, giddy at day's end, would look always to the large estate jutting sadly alone on the hill crest. This place we came to call "The Villa," and nights, after the dusk had extinguished its rosy light, we whispered together in bed about the imagined inhabitants, telling each other stories as surely as if they were facts.

My sister populated The Villa with characters one might find in royal and ancient lineages: a handsome Marquis whose flesh was the colour of cinnamon, his elegant regal lady wife, and their four beautiful children, all sons, and each blessed by the stars under which he was born.

Her descriptions, filled with such devotion and care, caused my heart sorrow, for we both knew already that

these fragile creations of our tired musings must suc-
cumb to the greatest suffering so that we, their creators,
might be freed from our own.

Yet, still, it was I who first breathed the curse upon
them, for no one has a claim to unending bliss, and as I
laboured in the fields like a beast, I made the lady my
first victim, sending a disease so ravishing to her door
that, in the end, she would have destroyed her entire
family, set her beloved villa to flames, in order to escape
the pain of her blackening body and the sympathy of
those whose lives would continue long after her own
had ended.

Her children grieved her death, taking their first sips
of suffering before they had grown strong enough to
endure its withering poison, while her husband, the
Marquis, himself fell ill with despair.

My sister brought the Marquis a physician from the
town over the hill, who summoned him back from the
brink of death. And yet, still, I would not let him rise
from his bed fully whole as he had fallen, for all resur-
rections must be paid for, and the cost of his, I determined, must be high.

My sister protested. She refused to proceed with the
stories if I would not allow her some salvation. But as
the heat of the summer grew more punishing and sweat
rolled from our blistering scalps to our heels, my sister
allowed me my way, and the Marquis, never regaining
strength of mind, was locked up, his children left to the
care of a serving maid who felt no affection for them,
and in this way they grew as my sister and myself grew

from one year to the next, helpless and at the mercy of fate.

Days joined to years and my sister and I bent to the earth, assuaging our ravaged hands in mud, gathering stories like stone, for we could cry over the sad lives of the orphans as we toiled and dwelt in the centre of this sweet flowering compassion.

But too soon the day arrived that my sister was carried from the fields. Her body crooked, her cool face plundered with scars.

Alone in bed I spoke to her silent ghost, for it seemed she had taken the stories away with her, leaving me nothing but empty desire. Cold nights hung open and infinite and the harshness of day snapped unrelenting and heavy with the burden of work never ending.

The sky sank low upon me, clouds filled my nose and throat. My legs trembled and threatened to snap, for as much as I looked to the villa, my mind created nothing but darkness.

And then, one day, when I could stand the emptiness no longer, I looked up at the villa, and knew I must make a pilgrimage there. I gathered my few belongings, collected small quantities of cheese and bread for the journey and set off before sunrise, walking steadily till dusk.

The road that wound and looped its way toward the villa was like a dream, growing suddenly close, then distant, curving and eternal, and I thought I might never reach my destination when the first evening fell and the blackness of night claimed my vision.

I slept in a rocky ditch, for I could not see my way to the soft blanket of leaves beyond the roadside, and cold moved deeply into my shivering bones and stopped my heart, it seemed, for all night long I slept as if dead. And when light came again to the sky, I was surprised to wake and find myself still living.

For miles I followed the road, high and low, past villages that sprung up and vanished as if they were all nothing more than illusion, and trees reached out with pointed wooden fingers, as if they too were eager for me to arrive.

My feet walked and walked, with soles badly torn, carrying my tired body forward into the sun, and so I continued walking through the night and through the day until finally the gates of the villa arose before me, like magical doors leading away from the world.

Immediately, I noticed the rose bushes just inside the gates. They were overgrown, untended, and I thought how the lady had cared for these bushes before her death. How she had selected them, planted them, nurtured them, and once long ago now had cut their magnificent blooms to wear in her hair and set in elegant crystal vases.

In the distance, I could see a man. His hair was the colour of rosewood, and though young he walked with a limp, as if time had burrowed into his bones; and I wondered who he might be, for in our story the servants all had vanished, and the boys, but for the youngest who was still just a child, had succumbed to sorrow and illness, and no one else lived there.

The man approached the gate making no secret that my presence displeased him, and then I explained I had been walking many days, and he saw I was exhausted and that my feet bled, and he led me through the courtyard where statues once whole and regal stood, and then down a long pathway of jagged stone until we reached the threshold of his home.

The surroundings, with the exception of the rose bushes at the gate, looked unfamiliar to me. The house itself, it seemed, had undergone renovation in more prosperous times—perhaps just before the lady's death, I thought. But now it was no longer new. The roof needed repair. The chimney, I could see, had lost several bricks, and the man confided to me that he had shut down an entire wing of the house because he could not afford its upkeep.

He gave me food and a place to rest, and when the following morning arrived his manner toward me had undergone such a transformation that he asked if I wished to spend another night, for he was a lonely man and rarely had company.

So often, throughout that first day, I wanted to ask him about his history, if he had known the people who had lived here before him, how he had come to be the possessor of this estate, but these questions seemed somehow unspeakable, and so instead I listened to his soothing voice present pictures of lands he had been to and places I would never see.

And then that night he came to my bed, his face hot and brilliant with tears and sweat, and when his mouth touched mine, I knew immediately everything, for the taste of grief on his lips was as fresh as the day I had painted it there, and though tragedy had so rapidly aged him and his surroundings, there was no doubt this man was the youngest orphan son of the unfortunate couple who had once lived so blissfully here.

I allowed myself to become his lover, feeding upon the certain knowledge of my creation, and containing within myself all the poignant barbs of melancholy I could hold. We lived together for a year in a slow soundless dream until my lover, ignorant of the nature of our union, sent me home.

The fields had become graves, and those who had survived the plague had become strangers. I walked through the dusty abandoned roads like a ghost, slept near the bones of my sister. The villa blazed beyond the sloping mountains, far above the village, and all the stories of its history that once had filled me vanished to nothing.

The disease that had claimed so many came to sit upon my shoulder, and I welcomed it. But it left me living, though barely alive.

I travelled to the villa again, for now it was the only path I knew, yet I hoped in my weakness I would not arrive there. But the path moved this time like quick rushing lava under my hot feet, and the wind at my back propelled me so that it seemed my frail body flew and I was untouched by the measure of days.

I needed no one to open the crumbling gate, as the tired lock had rusted to nothing, and the heavy hinges collapsed into ashes of red.

The rose bushes no longer existed, but patches of wild grass jutted between the cracks and fissures of stone, and I crept toward the old estate feeling small and hungry, wondering if my lover still might live.

The house itself was now a ruin. Broken bricks bordered its walls, and in many places the roof had given way to the punishing elements.

I stood surveying the property, recalling my sister and happier times when the estate was filled with joy and the promise of future, how we made the lady dance with her husband in the moonlight, and the children play.

Vague noises rang from within the house now. Sounds both wild and plaintive. Then I saw him, my lonely lover, the orphaned son, rushing toward me. I opened my arms to receive his embrace, believing only there could I hold the exquisite human suffering I had made of him, but when he reached my arms, it was no longer him. His flesh had turned coarse, his face grown twisted, nails had transformed to claws, teeth to daggers.

Inside the ruins of the villa, I found a corner where my wounded body sank and the moaning world beyond could no longer reach me. A place where I could rest and sleep, where grey stone walls could crumble to dust, blow free in the wind without cause or consequence, and the stories of my youth would no longer plague me.